CELTIC
TIES

A Lizzy O'Malley Mystery

CELTIC TIES

Kelly Running

Celtic Ties

Lake Oswego, Oregon

www.kellyrunningmysteries.com

ISBN: 978-0-692-73063-8

Editing and design by Indigo Editing & Publications.

This book is dedicated to my mother.

It seems to me that I saw things before I actually saw them.

—EDNA O'BRIEN

Contents

Chapter 1

The Crossing

FATIGUE. JET LAG. I NEEDED to power through it. I was thousands of miles away from home—in fact, I wasn't sure where home was anymore. Crossing the street, I felt myself pulled back with a sharp snap by someone as a bus whizzed past me. Adrenaline shot through me. My heart pounded in my chest. *I almost died. Traffic drives on the opposite side of the street. I'm in Ireland.* Turning around, I viewed a muscled man with piercing blue eyes. He wore a crucifix around his neck and a diamond stud in his ear. *Black Irish. And so handsome.*

I extended my shaking hand.

"You're fine, it is," he said.

I looked up the street and watched a puff of exhaust backfire from the double-decker bus that had almost killed me. I composed myself with a nervous laugh. My hands were still shaking.

"Lucky for you I came along," he said. "I was on a bit of an errand when you tried to walk in front of a bus."

I grimaced.

"Would you like to get a cup of tea and go for some *craic*?" he asked.

"Oh, I don't do drugs."

"*Craic*," he said with a laugh. He had a tiny gap between his teeth. "It means fun. Let's have a bit of it. And, please, call me Cormac."

"Lizzy," I said.

"American, by your accent. Lovely."

The summer evening light danced through the trees of Fitzgerald Park. In the corner of it was a family-friendly café painted a warm tangerine. We sat there and watched as children played in the still-warm Irish night.

I inhaled the rich scent. I was as enchanted with Cormac as I would have been to see fairies dance.

When twilight came, Cormac asked, "I'll see you Sunday?"

Really? I thought. *He's a handsome Irish guy. In Ireland! But we only met a couple hours ago.*

My internal talk is often like a volley in a tennis match.

But this feels right, I thought.

"I've got to get to bed," I said.

Cormac's blue eyes danced in the fading light after my Freudian-esque suggestion. I'd already pictured an Irish cottage and a stone wall with sheep.

"I've got to get back to the bed and breakfast and get some sleep." I put an extra emphasis on the word *sleep*.

"Sleep it is," Cormac said as he walked me back to my lodging.

At the door, he leaned in and kissed me goodnight. When I came up for air, he said, "Sleep well, Lizzy O'Malley, from the United States. I'll see you Sunday."

Inside the B & B, I was a teenager again. I watched through the front window as Cormac disappeared down the street after our electrifying kiss. I had butterflies in my stomach like the first time Ronnie Parker kissed me in grade school.

There was a common area in the bed and breakfast with a kitchen table, fresh flowers, and a refrigerator for guests to use. I had some white wine in the refrigerator, so I poured myself a glass and took a sip. I rummaged through the crisper for some Irish cheese to go with my wine.

This looks delicious. I took out a white cheddar and cut two wedges. Still foraging, I found rosemary crackers in the cupboard that someone had left. *A feast,* I thought. Smiling, I choked on my second sip of wine as I pulled out the business card from my pocket that Cormac had given me when he'd asked to see me on Sunday. I hadn't looked at it because, infatuated, I couldn't take my eyes off of him at the time.

"We'll meet here," he said as he pressed the card into my hand, and I had allowed his tongue to go places in my mouth where few men have gone before.

Now wine shot out of my nose. I took the card and tossed it, disgusted, on the table:

St. Patrick's Church
Lower Glanmire Road
Cork, Ireland
Parish Priest: Cormac O'Connor

"I need to quit making out with priests," I said to the empty room.

Chapter 2
Mass Matters

I WISHED I'D LISTENED TO my brain instead of my hormones. After all, Cormac was a priest. And he'd French kissed me like a boyfriend. I watched as devout Catholic women worked the beads on their rosaries with arthritic hands in St. Patrick's Church. They prayed: "Hail Mary, full of grace…"

Am I sniffing at forbidden fruit?

I scanned the faces of the faithful—mothers, fathers, and children in the pews. Cormac was at the back of the church in the narthex with altar servers and another, prune-like priest. Cormac looked even more handsome. In his priestly robes he was distinguished, traditional. Missing was the diamond stud from his earlobe. The Celtic cross tattoo on his arm was covered by his holy robes.

I'd sat near the aisle of the church so I could get a good view. *Yes*, I thought. *You're taking a bite out of the apple. But even if Eve is such a tart, isn't Adam part of the problem too?*

I clasped my hands to my head. *Think holy thoughts.*

Cormac saw me from the back of the narthex, in his green and white-colored robes, and smiled. *I'm not thinking holy thoughts. I really need to go to confession.*

Rapid-fire thinking was like a mental vortex. *Is it a mortal sin if I confess to a priest my fantasies? Is it a venial or mortal sin to think like this? I think it is mortal. That's the really bad kind of sin.*

Cormac held the *Book of the Gospels* and started down the aisle. The altar boys followed him like miniature priests.

What happened next occurred without any premonition on my part. No tingling sensation. No metallic taste in my mouth. These were the psychic signs I'd inherited from my maternal side of the family, and I didn't feel any of them—maybe because I was in a church, or because the threat wasn't directed toward me. A haggard-faced man stood in front of me in the dark-oak pew that was worn from decades of faithful attendance, and I caught the glint of metal. Too soon I realized it was a knife under his ragged coat, and he lunged toward Cormac. There was a divine moment between present and future when there was no sound. Then a woman screamed.

Ashen-faced congregants rushed out the back of the church through the narthex. I checked my own urge to flee and watched Cormac, who moved like a street fighter as he wrestled with the man with the knife until it finally dropped to the ground. Once he'd disarmed the man, Cormac kicked his legs out from under him and dropped him to the floor, quick as lightning. Spittle spewed from the attacker's mouth as he ranted, swore, and vowed to kill Cormac. As we listened to the psychopath, the color in the perpetrator's face drained, and in a final, chilling moment, he turned his head and stared at me—eyes open, without blinking.

At this point, the ones who were still in the church, many helping Cormac, said they had never seen this man before. One man speculated that he was a "blow-in." That's an Irish expression for someone who has moved from another town. I was about to leave when the *gardaí*, the Irish police, entered the church and told everyone to sit and wait for questioning.

I briefly talked with the police, explaining that I was a friend of an intern at University College Cork, an American, and traveling to the Beara Peninsula to visit a distant relative. After that, I was allowed to leave. I had absolutely been in the wrong place at the wrong time. I vowed not to see Cormac again. I knew the signs of bad karma.

Chapter 3

Violation

AFTER A CUP OF HERBAL tea in the University College Cork campus commons, I headed toward my room in the dormitories where I'd checked in the day before. The regular university students had left for the summer, and I was leasing a dorm room by the week. It was nice to be closer to campus, in a fairly modern building, only blocks away from the main campus. Except today because when I got to my dorm room, the door was hanging open, and I remembered having locked it. I thought I had the wrong room, so I double-checked the door number.

It's my room.

Stepping inside, I saw a light shining from under the bathroom door.

I hadn't left a light on.

As I looked around the other side of my bed, I saw that every article of my clothing—bras, panties, and shoes—was on the ground. My new wool scarf was twisted around my pillow like it had been strangled. *Who harbors such anger toward a fluffy headrest?*

Peeking inside the bathroom, I saw that my toiletries were trashed on the floor. On the mirror, in my bright-pink flamingo lipstick, something was written in Irish.

I backed out of the room and rushed to summon the warden (the title for the overseer of the dormitories). Aidan was a thin man with gray hair tied in a ponytail. As I paced, he tried to occupy me with the lyrics of some Bob Dylan songs. He knew every line of every song. I knew only a few refrains.

When an Inspector Keating arrived, I gave him a complete accounting—except the part about Cormac. The inspector had faded red hair and keen eyes and looked to be somewhere in his forties. When he asked me if anything was missing, my face turned red as we went to my room and I sorted through my clothes, including my Valentine-red Victoria Secret bra and heart-decorated undies from the floor.

"I don't think so," I said, blushing.

"Do you have any idea who might have done this?"

Keating looked long and hard at me like I was keeping a secret. And, of course, I had omitted the part about the errant priest.

"Because that message in the mirror is a warning," he added as he looked up from his notepad to watch me with his hazel-colored eyes as I tossed my clothes on the bed.

"Translated?" I asked as I dangled my black bra from my finger. "What does it say on the mirror?"

Curiosity killed the cat. But if I wanted to solve this puzzle, I needed information.

"It's a rather graphic threat, really. In Irish it means to mind your fucking business. Pardon the vulgar word." He looked down at his notes. "But it's serious, and an American in Ireland shouldn't be sniffing around the Troubles in Cork." Keating said the word *Troubles* with extra emphasis and looked over at the warden.

"I don't know anything about the Irish Troubles." *And I'm not going to talk to you. I'll save that for the confessional, not the gardaí.* I didn't like cops, not American or Irish.

"Maybe she should change rooms—just as a precaution," Keating suggested when the silence in the room began to feel like we were sitting in a forest waiting for mushrooms to grow.

"I'll see to it, then," Aidan agreed.

Keating waited in silence for a minute longer. When he realized that I was still going to be tight lipped, he turned away. Over his shoulder he said, "If you think of anything else, give me a ring."

I took all my clothes and walked down the hall to the washers and dryers. I threw darks in one machine and whites in another, and then I started up the washers and sat as I listened to water fill and the agitation cycle begin. *That's how I feel.* The clothes rotated in the water in the low-water, energy-efficient machine. Feeling violated, I at least wanted to clean the clothes that some scumbag had touched. My pent-up emotions exploded, and I took my bag—the one that I'd been carrying with me since I'd arrived in Ireland, the one that I'd taken through international customs, the one that I'd been carrying when Cormac saved me from the speeding bus—and I threw it across the room in a rash and wanton act of anger and self-pity.

Clank. "What was that?" I said to the empty room. *Was that a clank or a clunk? What is it that I have in there?* I systemically began to expunge the contents—every pocket, pouch, and do-hickey—*zip, zip, zip.* When I unzipped one of the outer side pockets, I found what had produced that sound against the wall: a small metal box.

11

Inside was a rosary. But it was shorter than the ones that I'd seen before. It had ten wooden beads and an eleventh, raw, uncut stone. A cross dangled from one end, with a ring—large enough to fit a finger. And I knew it didn't belong to me.

Chapter 4

River Lee

My job, at least for a few days, was to assist my friend, Mary Moore, with a bit of stage consulting. She worked as an intern at the University College Cork, making the set for the summer play production, *Macbeth*, at the Granary Theater. Mary and I had met two years ago, while she was visiting her Irish-American cousins who lived in Oregon; she and I worked together on a set at the Lakewood Theater in Lake Oswego, Oregon.

"If you visit Ireland, see me," she'd said in her thick accent on the last day of work. She was like the sister I never had.

Now, in Ireland, Mary had invited me to Professor Malone's two-hour lecture beginning at nine o'clock in the morning. I stopped at the Bagel Box, a coffee and bagel shop on the way to class in the *Aula Maxima*, the great hall. I ordered the strawberry-and-banana smoothie and a breakfast bagel with egg and melted cheese. I paid in euros, got my order number, and sat at one of the outside tables since the weather had been unseasonably hot in Cork. I didn't know the exact temperature because when I looked for the weather report, I got Celsius instead of Fahrenheit, and it was never worth the effort to make the conversion. I had on a tank top—a yellowish lime green that actually looked good with my auburn hair and skin—a black skirt, and TOMS shoes. I also wore a dangling silver bracelet and earrings that I'd gotten in Sedona, Arizona. I was always drawn to jewelry. Actually, it was like an addiction. I wore the sparkling sapphire ring from my short relationship with a Sedona cop, which was a disaster and needed to be left in the past. I didn't want to see Officer John Hall again. *I shouldn't have let him get close to me.* I shook off the ruminations.

Crossing the River Lee on the pathway to campus, I stopped on the bridge to watch the dark water roil over moss-covered stones. I briefly considered seeing Cormac again to ask about the rosary and what Keating had insinuated, but my intuition knew to leave well enough alone.

I'd found the hall of stones on the first day I had been on campus, a few days ago. On that first time through the stone-filled corridor, I couldn't pass by without stopping to look at the rock relics of the past engraved with an ancient language. These stones, called the Ogham, originated from all over Ireland. Each was etched with an ancient form of early writing. Historians believed the stones were used as burial markers or boundary markers—or maybe both.

One in particular caught my attention—it was marked number twenty-five. It had been found in a bog. The sign read *6 Charraig an Ghiolla Co/Chorai from Carrigagulla, Co. Cork.* The markings looked like a bear claw scratched on it. It translated to the family name of Dovetti. That sounded Italian instead of Irish to me.

Who marks property in a bog?

It made me think of bodies engulfed in mist-veiled, foggy places.

There's something about these stones. Something that inspires me and defies time.

I still had time to kill before class, so I walked to the Honan Chapel on the campus. Entering, I dripped a bit of holy water on my forehead, signed myself with the cross, and slipped into a pew. My father had taken me to mass when I was little. It was a seed of faith that never had enough light to grow, however. But now, in the chapel, it felt like it could take root.

There was another person in front of me. Even looking at the back of his head, I realized he resembled someone I'd met before, but I couldn't quite place him. I finished some quick intentions—for my deceased Aunt Thelma and my father—and then emerged from the cool, dark chapel into the sunlight.

I made my way to class and sat in the back of the room with several students, all of whom were waiting for Professor Malone's lecture. Mary was already there. We chatted, and as more time passed, I doodled on a pad of paper. More students arrived, drinking coffee, even though the classroom had a sign that clearly read *No food or beverages allowed*. My doodles turned into drawings of the arched classroom window and its leaded glass with clear panes.

Malone was late. One student left and headed down the hallway toward the Ogham stones. I looked at my watch. It was twenty minutes past the hour. A few students looked to Mary, and then she looked at me. Mary knew that I could teach. She urged me with a tug at my elbow. "You'll be lovely," Mary said to me in a whisper.

"Introduce yourself, and with your American accent, you'll dazzle," she added.

Why not?

I cleared my throat, stood up in front of the class, introduced myself as a theater consultant, and talked about my brother's theater in Sedona, Arizona. I'd designed and painted the set for *A Midsummer Night's Dream* a month ago. I talked about the faux stone pillars in the theater and how I'd achieved the paint technique. I explained how the design was in keeping with the original Globe, *Shakespeare's* Globe, and how the reconstructed theater in England used the same process. "It is as if it was designed from the original in 1599. The pillars look like stone, but it is a clever paint deception. Shakespeare was known to commit trickery on stage sets."

At that moment, Professor Malone entered the classroom, a ragged look on his face. He apologized for being late and took his lecture notes out of his briefcase. I quickly took my seat, and he nodded at Mary and at me. He was distinguished and academic; however, about five minutes into his lecture—about Shakespeare and how he wrote when the theater was closed due to the plague—the professor abruptly stopped.

He sat down on his chair and buried his hands in his head. Finally, when he looked up, he cleared his throat, and said, "You'll surely hear when you leave class." The room was silent. "The gardaí are looking for..."

"Mary, Jesus, and Joseph, what's happened?" Mary blurted out.

"The gardaí are looking for a body in the river on campus."

It would be silly to jump to the conclusion that the body the police were looking for in the River Lee was Cormac. *It's too Shakespearean,* I thought. But part of me believed it. A part of me *felt* like it was true. As I pondered the meaning of the professor's statement, the hairs on my arm stood on end. Professor Malone continued his lecture, talking about the Globe Theater, but I was lost in my own thoughts about a priest's body and the murky water of the River Lee.

Mary and I, along with several other students from the class, walked down the campus pathway toward the main entrance gate. It was the same direction that Mary and I would take walking toward the theater when we worked on the sets. We didn't get very far down the path before we were stopped by the gardaí. A crowd had gathered there along with official vehicles inside the main gate, where iron chains normally stopped traffic.

An enormous old tree grew from the banks of the River Lee, draped over the dark, flowing water. The River Lee splits in two as it meanders through Cork. Some people in the city call it an Irish Venice, because Cork was once in the marshes and boats floated up to the old homes in the city. These homes had a boathouse underneath the main house, where the owners would moor their vessels before climbing up to the main house. Now the River Lee's boat homes have been converted to apartments.

A ripple of gossip floated through the crowd. I heard "priest's clothing." Mary was speaking Irish to a student next to her.

"They think it's a priest from St. Patrick's," she said to me and signed herself with the cross. "There's a suicide note, nailed to that tree."

I looked over to where Mary was pointing, and the tree's dark boughs, draped over the river, swayed in a light breeze.

Chapter 5

Memorial Mass

I ENTERED THE CROWDED CHURCH for Cormac's memorial mass. "It's a memorial mass instead of a funeral mass because there's no body," Mary whispered to me.

My father's side of the family was Catholic. My mother, long disappeared from my life, was purported to be crazy. My Aunt Thelma had raised me. She had been a spiritualist and the *real* psychic in the family.

I had on a one-size-fits-all black jersey dress in one of those wonder materials that never wrinkles. I also wore a gray cashmere cardigan sweater and black ballet flats. I'd combed my fingers through my auburn waves and checked my reflection in the window glass before I stepped through the heavy oak doors and entered the vestibule. Not surprisingly, a sea of black clothing had invaded the church.

I gazed at the candles that burned on the altar while I eavesdropped on conversations and smelled the spicy scent of incense. *That's the same scent I smelled on Cormac when we met.*

An Irish flute played in a soft lilt, and people stood on cue as the old priest, the one I'd seen with Cormac before, walked toward the altar.

At the end of the memorial mass—which I don't really remember because I kept ruminating about Cormac—I was brought back to the present when the priest stood at the altar and told us to go in peace and love.

Once again in the sunlight on the steps outside, Mary and I turned to walk back to her car. She had given me a lift, and she also wanted us to go to the wake. Mary was a member of St. Patrick's and insisted that it was only right that we should go to both.

If she hadn't invited me, I wouldn't have gone. But she was my host and I was her guest. She gave me the Irish, green-eyed look that said that I *should* go.

I had the antique rosary hidden on me. I couldn't leave it in my dorm room because I figured that it would only be a matter of time before someone came for it again. I couldn't understand its value or purpose—why did I have it? I figured I might be able to gather a clue at the wake. When I examined it, the rich patina of the rosary was lovely, and the rough stone glimmered in a bright light, even under the grime of age. I'd even considered turning it into a piece of jewelry if I couldn't find the owner, but a part of me knew that wouldn't be right.

Suddenly, Mary lowered her voice. "Watch what happens," she whispered. "The gardaí won't be able to stop it."

Several uniformed Irish police were scattered outside the church. Before I could ask a question, three men in the distance, away from the crowd—faces covered with black hoods—took out rifles and shot three rounds into the air. For a minute, I thought I should hit the ground, but the police didn't move. Neither did anyone else.

Reading my startled expression, Mary ushered me down the church stairs with a little, quick shove. She hustled me into her car, in the opposite direction of the men who were dressed in black balaclavas. I looked behind me as the crowd blended into a huge human wave.

"It's rumored that Cormac led a double life," she whispered.

You betcha. I was still too embarrassed to confide in Mary that I'd met Cormac before. I was ashamed about how he'd made me feel when his warm lips were on mine—oh, and the tingling sensation I still got from thinking about him now.

Stop it, stop it!

Still in a low voice, Mary continued, "Cork has a few tatters of rebellion—the Troubles. Some still yearn for a united Ireland. Some factions take a cut from drug trafficking and claim it's money for the fight." She stopped and added, "But drugs have brought grief to Cork."

Drugs always bring misery.

Automobiles were parked on both sides of the road at Cormac's brother's house. The house was whitewashed and set back from the road. As we parked, a dark-blue metallic BMW pulled up beside Mary's car. The four occupants of the automobile wore black and gave me a steely stare.

Mary smiled and waved.

"What's with the dark greeting?" I asked. *Did I trample a local custom?* "For the most part, I'd always been welcomed everywhere," I added.

"Pay no mind to the likes of them," she answered and kept her smile intact until the occupants had made their way down the pathway toward the front of the house.

Looking down the road, I spied the local cemetery filled with stone Celtic crosses.

Irish-lace curtains floated in the breeze as we approached the house from the gravel pathway. Mary and I entered the house, through an arched doorway, and the scent of fuchsias rippled through the air.

I don't think I need to stay long.

I was about to tell Mary that I'd take a cab back—I wasn't enjoying the negative vibes—when a dark-haired, muscled man in a black suit, black shirt, and black tie—with features much like Cormac's—stepped into the room that we'd just entered. I sucked in air. He could have been Cormac's twin. I blinked and looked again.

No, I thought, *not twin.* This man's nose had a little tiny twist to it—like it had been broken and reset, but not by a doctor—and a tiny scar raced down the right side of his cheek. Where Cormac was a polished, oh-my-god-he-is-good-looking man, this version was more rugged.

Maybe from street fights?

The handsome Cormac look-alike came over to Mary and me. The room had filled with people, and there was a table covered with food (straight from the English Market would be my guess): meats, cheeses, olives, thick-crusted breads, herb-sprinkled breads, fresh black cherries, raspberries, and fresh strawberries with whipped cream.

I almost forgot my manners but redeemed myself with a handshake. That's when recognition wracked my brain. I'd seen this different version of Cormac before. This was the same man I'd seen in the dim chapel light at the University College Cork campus the last time I'd been there.

I could sense that he recognized me too. "Please stay," he said as he excused himself. He walked over to the prune-like priest who had just come through the open front door.

Mary, watching, came closer to me and said, "Watch. No one has taken a bite of food from the table."

Now that she mentioned it, the gourmet-food-filled table had gone untouched—and it was hard to ignore.

"Irish custom," she explained. "No one can eat at a wake until the priest is served."

Sure enough, a woman came over to the priest and led him through the buffet and then over to a smaller table set with an Irish-linen tablecloth, crystal, and china. Once he was seated, along with a handful of guests, several people took plates and heartily filled them. The others sat down and started to eat.

Mary grinned. "Tradition," she said as an explanation.

I had to use two hands for my plate because it was so heavy with food. Somehow, I found my appetite. There was an open table in another room, and when I sat down there, I was promptly handed a pint of Guinness.

"I met Cormac," I finally confessed to Mary while drinking my pint. "He saved my life after I arrived in Cork." I recited the clean version. I kept out the part about the kissing and the sexual tension that had sizzled between us.

"Liam is Cormac's brother," she whispered. "He's a professor of history at the university and..." She stopped, interrupted. I followed to where she was looking, above my forehead. That led me to spy Cormac's brother, Liam.

"You stayed," he said with a smile for both of us. "And I've seen you before on campus," he said to me. "Are you a student?"

"Consultant," I said. "I'm helping Mary with her internship," I added.

Mary conveniently stood up then, politely excused herself, and greeted some friends who'd just arrived. That left a place for him to sit down, and he didn't hesitate. I was ready to give Mary a glare when an old man sat close to us and launched into a loud story.

"Now, Mrs. O'Donnell succumbed to the fever, and when the doctor came, he told the family he was too late," the man said. He was dressed in tweed with ruddy cheeks—either from the strong sun in Cork the last couple of weeks, which had been unseasonably warm, or from the pints of Guinness he had consumed.

Everyone within earshot made the sign of the cross.

He continued without missing a beat. "So the family buried her. The problem was that Paddy forgot to remove her wedding band. You see, Paddy and his lads had too much to drink that night they buried Mrs. O'Donnell, and they'd forgotten to extract the ring. Her husband asked Paddy for it, so Paddy went to dig her up. But when he opened the casket, he found her fingernail scratches on the underside of the coffin—which meant, of course, that she wasn't dead when they buried her."

The air was still. Not even the lace curtains moved in the open windows. My heart skipped a beat.

"So," he waited with a pregnant Irish pause, "that's why Irish wakes go on for days—to make sure the dead are really departed!"

I choked on my Guinness.

Back at the dormitory, I found Aidan, the dormitory warden, in a chartreuse-colored chair in one of the common rooms, which smelled like cinnamon and sugar cookies. He was tidying up and said he wanted to make sure everything was fine and that I hadn't had any more unexpected visitors. He handed me a snickerdoodle cookie.

I thought about what I'd seen outside the funeral, and about what Mary had told me about the IRA and the country's factions. Aidan seemed like a good source for more information.

"Aidan," I said, "can you tell me a little about Ireland and the peace agreement?" I sat down in a chair next to him and pulled my hair into a ponytail. It felt liberating to get my hair off my neck.

"I'll give you the short version," he answered. "Otherwise, we'll be here all night."

He explained the events that led up to the 1916 Easter Rising. He told me how that political rebellion had been a failure at first—people barely listened while the proclamation was read—but the events that followed sparked the revolution. The members—after voluntarily surrendering—were executed. Patrick Pearse was the leader. That's when Aidan looked as if he could see legions of Irish ghosts in the room. "Pearse read the proclamation; he and his brother, who had no part in the uprising, were both executed. If you get up to Dublin sometime, you can go into the gaol—jail—and see the cell where he spent his final days and where the British executed him in the Kilmainham Gaol courtyard. His brother's name was William; he was two years younger than Patrick. Their mother lost both of her sons for the freedom of Ireland, and it broke her heart."

I had seen the graveyard at the back of the campus quad when I'd left the Bagel Box, and this seemed a good time to ask about it. I recalled seeing fresh flowers on the gravestones. "What's happened there?"

"Some of the campus belonged to Cork Gaol."

"You mean that gloomy building on the hill facing the River Lee?"

I recalled the stone façade of the jail, dark and grimy like the events that had occurred behind the closed doors—it was said that when the gaol was still active, there were three windows in the upper part of the jail where inmates were publicly hanged. I stifled a shiver as I thought about it. Underground tunnels were rumored to intersect with parts of the original building, along with the underbelly of Shannon Castle.

Aidan's eyes closed as he recited the names off the graves on the campus: "Maurice Moore, Patrick O'Sullivan, Patrick O'Mahony…"

He broke off at three, but I knew there were more.

"It seems I've gotten a little carried away." He stood from his chair and stretched his legs. "I'll be saying goodnight now." As he was about to walk toward the evening twilight, he turned back toward me.

"Nothing has happened for days," I said.

Aidan smiled. "Keep safe."

The door rang with a sharp *clang* as he pulled it shut.

I crept on tiptoes to my dorm room. *The Irish can be really morose.* Unlocking my door, I breathed a sigh of relief. Everything looked okay. No torn-up articles of clothing. Nothing was disturbed. It was just like it was supposed to be.

I sat down on my bed. At times like this, when my independent streak gets slapped around a bit, I realized how much I missed my brother, Ryan O'Malley, and my dog—a black Labrador, Karma—who was with me in Sedona when I worked with my brother as a stage manager. I wished I was back there now, even though I knew it wasn't my permanent home. I had to return to Oregon by the end of summer in order to sell my Aunt Thelma's house in Manzanita, on the Oregon coast. Karma was boarding with a friend there, waiting for me.

Thinking about everything that had happened, my face grew flushed, but I wasn't going to cry. I took a washcloth from the bathroom, rinsed it with cold water, and wiped off my face. Then I did what any homesick American does in Ireland to recalibrate: I watched a half hour of *Judge Judy* on the tiny television in my room. After eating some serious leftover snacks, I could breathe again. Tomorrow, I planned to get temporary anxiety relief: I would get out and—shop.

Chapter 6
Stress-Relief Shopping

On Patrick Street I found just what I needed—clothes and jewelry. First I found a red dress that made my figure look like Marilyn Monroe's. The dress was tight; I'd gained a few pounds with mornings of porridge and evening suppers of fish chowder and brown bread. I spun around in the dressing room and decided to *buy*. The next two purchases were shirts, black and rose colored, to wear with leggings or jeans. I was feeling better already. Things were looking up for me. *Why do I worry about everything?* I allowed the emotions of my dorm-room intrusion to dissolve.

With my purchases firmly tucked under my arm, I walked outside into a fine rain. The weather had changed. After walking a half block, I found a storefront with silver jewelry. It caught my eye, and I could feel the familiar rush of shopping adrenaline coursing through my veins. Jewelry was my shot in the arm when I needed an emotional pick-me-up.

Stepping inside the shop, I spotted the jewelry maker working at his craft bench. As I looked through the cases, a necklace with a salmon charm, a Celtic design, caught my eye. The salmon was a powerful symbol in the Pacific Northwest too. A sign by the necklace read that the salmon symbolizes fertility; it fights against all odds to make the pilgrimage to the stream in which it spawned; in the Celtic tradition, the salmon symbolizes knowledge and wisdom. I wasn't interested in fertility, at least at this point in my life, so I dismissed the necklace and flashed to the silver dangle earrings that had just caught my eye.

I want.

I was getting my receipt for my earring purchase, along with the VAT form, when the jewelry maker's expression changed. I thought that I'd done something wrong; I didn't know what, so I checked my receipt again. Everything looked in order, but when I looked up, I followed his gaze over my shoulder. Two men, dressed in black, stood on either side of the entrance.

I feel trouble.

Don't follow me, I thought. *Please, sweet Jesus, don't.* My eye began to twitch and the hairs on my arm stood on end. Then I got that metallic taste in my mouth, and I knew it was trouble. I have a sixth sense that goes off at times like this. It has saved my life several times. I had walked about ten steps out the door when the jewelry maker shut and locked it behind me. Then he put a CLOSED sign in the window.

Strange. Very strange.

Chapter 7
Family Matters

During my uneventful bus ride back to my dorm room, I tried not to think about the dark feeling that I'd gotten from the men in the store. Besides, I had to get ready for my appointment. Aunt Thelma had left directions for me in her last will and testament. I was to meet a solicitor—an Irish attorney—that my Uncle Callaghan had recommended to me.

The solicitor's secretary, a woman with ginger-colored hair wearing a brown tweed suit and a cream-colored silk blouse with a crimson scarf, sat at a desk in the lobby. Mr. McDonough's name was stenciled in gold-leaf letters in etched glass behind her.

Smiling, she asked me to follow her into Mr. McDonough's inner office.

The solicitor sat in front of a backdrop of bookcases filled with tomes. Distinguished, he had brown hair and a neatly trimmed beard with white whiskers poking through the reddish-brown ones.

He shook my hand in greeting.

"I've heard a great deal about you from your uncle. He asked me to help in any way I could, and I assured him that I would. Your great-aunt's request was that you find and meet with a relative on the remote Beara Peninsula. Which, by the way, is a part of Ireland filled with mysticism and magic."

"I intend to go next weekend."

"Splendid. If you have a chance, take part in the solstice festivities there. There's also a copper mine museum. If you have the time, I'd recommend it. You shouldn't have trouble finding a place to stay, but I'll give you the name of a bed and breakfast in Eyeries just in case." He jotted down a few lines on the back of his business card and handed it to me. "People say that once you visit the mystical Beara, you'll want to go back."

There was a quick rap on the door. An exquisite woman walked in to join us; she wore an expensive-looking pink silk blouse and a black wool skirt that accentuated her tiny waist. Her long, coarse, strawberry-blond hair flowed from under a wool beret tipped fashionably to one side.

"Ms. O'Malley, this is Fiona Kennedy, private investigator. She found your relative on the Beara."

The woman said, "She's well known in Eyeries and on the Beara. Her house sits up on the hillside with a lovely view of the bay, and she's an oracle."

"A psychic?"

"Yes, she's very talented. Catholic priests even venture out to meet and visit her. She always convinces them to sit for a reading. She's reputed to tell the future with stones." Fiona paused for a minute, glancing at her notes. "So, when are you leaving for the Beara?"

"Very soon, I hope."

"Brilliant."

The solicitor interjected. "I have a slight word of caution. Some families don't like Americans looking into their Irish heritage because

Irish law allows emigrated relatives to still claim a part of the family land; you can understand how many are wary about a family member they didn't know existed. You have a claim to property if a family link is legally established."

I let Fiona and the solicitor know I wasn't interested in Irish property, thanked them, and got up to leave. As I turned to exit the office, I felt an icy-cold draft in the doorway like I'd walked headfirst into a ghost. I turned around suddenly.

"Did you forget something?" the solicitor asked me.

"No," I said. "I felt…" Now I wasn't sure what I'd felt. A chill down my neck. A feeling like the room temperature had dropped about ten degrees.

"Just, thank you for your help," I said as I turned to leave his office again. At that moment, I yearned for the warmth of the sun on my face.

Luckily, the sun had come out. As I walked to catch the bus, I stopped for a while and watched the River Lee as it flowed toward the ocean. This dull ache in Ireland was palpable. It was implied in every place and every surname: so many people separated by the great hunger and emigration—for people left behind and the ones that never returned. Ghosts of the past and ghosts of the future.

Chapter 8

Liam's Lift

My solution for a ride to the Beara—which was a dilemma because of its remoteness—came as the result of a casual conversation in the cafeteria a couple of days after the wake. I had gone for a quick cup of coffee between classes. I planned to buy a cup for Mary, too. I spotted Liam, Cormac's brother, out of the corner of my eye. He came over while I stood in line waiting for the cashier. He had his own cup of coffee to purchase.

"I'll buy all three," he said to the cashier when we'd made it to the front of the line.

I was ready to protest his offer, but there was a line of caffeine-deprived and sleepy students behind us, so I accepted.

"Thank you," I said.

I poured cream into my cup at the station where people customized their coffee habit. Mary and I both liked cream.

Sprinkling sugar into his coffee, Liam said, "Are you enjoying Cork?"

"Yes," I said. "It's nice to spend time talking about the theater and sets and all that. Mary's getting ready for the next performance at the theater of *Macbeth*." Thinking about the play, I briefly flashed to the tragedy of Cormac and how the gardaí had lifted his clothes from the dark, murky water. *It's Shakespearean.*

I had both coffees in a tray, balanced in one hand, and was about to leave for class.

"Could we meet for lunch sometime?" Liam asked.

Caught off guard, I had to rebalance my tray of coffee cups. I recalled Mary's cat-grin when she'd looked between Liam and me at the wake.

"I'm leaving for the Beara in a few days," I said, "to find a relative in Eyeries. That's the primary reason for my time in Ireland."

Liam wasn't one to miss an opportunity. "I'm scheduled to take time off this weekend to drive to Glengarriff. It's close to Eyeries. It's no trouble to give you a lift. I'd enjoy the company." He'd said this with hardly a breath in between sentences.

I knew that *lift* was the Irish expression for ride. A *ride* in Ireland was a romp in the sack. I blushed and pushed that image from my mind. When I brought myself back to the offer at hand, it seemed like a perfect solution for my dilemma. *Kismet.*

"I'll pay for gas," I offered.

I'd researched my transportation options to the Beara earlier, and I'd found that trains didn't travel to the southernmost part of the peninsula. I hadn't wanted to impose on Mary any more than I had already. Now an answer had presented itself. I remembered how my Aunt Thelma would remind me that there were no coincidences.

I jotted down my dorm room address. Liam offered to pick me up on Saturday. On the way back to the classroom, I had to walk past the Ogham stones. I stopped because I thought I heard my name; however, when I turned around, there wasn't a living soul in the hallway of the stones.

Did the ancient Ogham stones whisper to me? Can stones talk? I'd been told that those people who take the time to hear—who put away the iPhones and the laptops—and pause long enough to listen could receive spirit messages. Kuruk, an old medicine man in Arizona, had taught me to communicate with the spirit world.

But this was new and different from before. My emerging psychometry—the ability to feel spiritual vibrations, which I'd experienced in Sedona—was like hearing stones speak.

Then it happened. One stone whispered a story about family property; another spoke about a marriage; still another about children lost to consumption, while another wept about hunger. Other stones chimed in like a Greek chorus about the families that had emigrated from Ireland and never returned.

Stop!

When I looked at my watch, I found only minutes had passed, although it felt much longer. I went to the women's toilet, the ladies' room, and splashed cold water on my face.

On my way back to class, an ancient limestone tried to whisper to me again, seeming desperate to tell its story.

Hush, stone. I have work to do.

Something was happening to me in this ancient land. The trip to meet my psychic relative in the Beara now seemed more urgent.

A last-minute change of plans before leaving for the Beara had me meeting Liam at his house instead; he didn't live far from campus.

When I arrived at Liam's house, I held the heavy door knocker in my hand, a twisted Celtic knot, and brought it down with a resounding *bang*. The door opened, and Liam stood in the doorway.

The light around him illuminated his aura. I could see the colors around him like an aurora borealis. Startled, I thought about how I'd seen an aura for the first time in Sedona about a month ago. It was like a fireworks display. Now, Liam's light bodies were clear and bright pink—the color of lust and desire. His aura was glowing from his base root chakra. I didn't need the cat-grin of Mary to confirm what Liam felt. I blushed—sometimes it's hard to be an emerging psychic.

He broke into an exquisite smile and invited me inside.

He's trying so hard.

"Lizzy," he said.

I loved the way my name sounded with an Irish accent.

The house was still; I wasn't sure if anyone lived with Liam or if anyone else shared his life.

"I thought we should have breakfast first." He motioned toward the kitchen. Eggs sizzled on the stovetop, and steamed porridge was ready, but it was the smell of fresh coffee that had me giddy. A coffee press sat on the table with a blue-and-white checked tablecloth. Fresh blackberries and raspberries spilled over the top of a delicate china bowl. Three kinds of Irish cheese were nestled together on a plate next to the berries. And beside it, fresh miniature pastries—almond and lemon filled.

"I'm dropping off my brother Michael at Castletownbere," he explained. "He should be here soon." A tinge of black entered his aura field as Liam French-pressed the coffee and poured me a cup.

I dipped my spoon into porridge topped with fresh Wexford strawberries and honey. "And I've added a stop to the Mass rock," he said excitedly.

He's really trying too hard.

There was a knock on the door. In came a man about six feet

tall—taller than Liam—and dressed in black, with a broad smile that could light up a room. His aura radiated brown, however.

Michael is only concerned about himself.

In the car, headed toward the Beara, we wound over green hills and pasture. There were large, empty homes along the sides of road in many places, some still with stickers on new windows. Liam told me they were left after the recession of 2008 swept through Ireland, part of the larger global recession, ending the boom years known as the Celtic Tiger.

I listened to him, but I mostly ruminated about my own personal events. Since I'd arrived in Cork, I'd been kissed by a wayward priest, witnessed a street fight in a Holy Mass, and suffered through a dorm room break-in that violated both my privacy and my Victoria's Secret underwear. Oh, and stones speak to me. *The least of my worries.*

We stopped for lunch at a restaurant in Glengarriff. It had once been a church and now was used as a coffee house and pub. Walking inside, we were greeted with a gloomy interior—it had a dark ambiance and a sense of despair.

We decided to sit outside at one of the four picnic tables, but even there, hushed stories, inaudible whispers, penetrated my consciousness. *Loss, mourning, death.* The stones of the church wanted to speak to me.

Hush, stones.

I turned my face toward the sun. We gazed at the sea—at the fishing boats particularly, light on the water, bound for the catch of the day. My order came, a grilled cheese and tomato sandwich. The sun nipped at my skin. There was a sense of foreboding from the eatery that I couldn't shake, but the sun seemed to block the dark stories that the place wanted to communicate.

When we were back on the highway, I felt a little lighter, and I even enjoyed watching the crews of men cutting the lush green growth away from the narrow roads.

"What's Mass rock?" I asked as we stopped again for the workers pruning the sides of the highway. I watched as sheep grazed in the distance and noticed that each one was painted with a stripe of a different color—pale blue, green, pink—and sometimes two colors.

"It's a stone altar where Catholics worshipped during the penal years—especially the sixteenth and seventeenth centuries. The British banned all forms of religious Catholic practice for the Irish back then," Liam said.

Mass rock was up the side of a hilly cliff. Sheep perched on the edge of the ridge.

"I've been so many times. I'm staying in the car," Michael said.

I started up the narrow trail. As I walked, the wind began to sing an ancient song, and I was transported, as if I'd walked here many times before. I felt about ten years old, and my clothes were dirty and tattered. I saw my other-life self—a child—looking toward the sea, toward some kind of danger or threat. I knew my mother and father had taught me that the consequences of practicing my religion were death. In the penal years, the price was high for attending mass—it was a clandestine act of defiance against the English—but week after week I went. I sucked in the cool air, and I knelt at the altar while the priest, ghostly, gave me the consecrated bread: "Kevia, the Body of Christ."

I knelt at the altar, ready to receive the host—the bread that had been transformed—when I felt a hand on my shoulder and jumped with a start.

It was Liam.

It was so real. Have I had more than one life?

This was like it had been in the Ogham stone hall—only minutes had passed since the last time I'd looked at my watch, but it felt like longer. I'd seen a priest and heard him call my name. I knew, without a doubt, that I'd walked this path countless times, although I rationally knew that I'd never been here before. *Psychic bipolar.*

"I'm going back to the car," I said to Liam abruptly.

The wind whistled softly at my back as I walked. When I was almost to the car, I turned and thought I saw a man on the cliff wearing dark clothing, but as I continued to gaze, he disappeared. I shook my head. *Irish ghosts.* Something about the Beara made the time between past and present fade.

I wonder if I'll be seeing the future? That, of course, had been my Aunt Thelma's specialty.

Back at the car, Michael was snoring.

I looked once more toward the cliff. *What happened there?*

Chapter 9

Eyeries

AFTER MANY TWISTS AND TURNS, driving down roads with whitewashed cottages and marveling at all the shades of green, we came to the town of Eyeries. Liam pulled up to buildings painted in lavender, blue, yellow, and orange.

"Irish pride," he said about the festively colorful buildings.

Well, I thought, *at least my Visa won't take a hit here.* There was a post office, a coffee shop, and a grocery store. That appeared to be the entire village. I wondered how I'd manage my need to shop—especially for jewelry.

"Anxious?" Liam asked, apparently reading my mind.

I doubt that I could explain what I was feeling. Especially after I'd seen an Irish priest's ghost at Mass rock.

"Well, then," he said when I didn't answer, "I'll pick you up in a week, next Saturday."

In the June light, with the sun around Liam's aura, I had a flash of Cormac as he leaned in to kiss me that first night we met. Michael was in the car with the engine idling and he looked at me as Liam danced around his indecision as to whether to kiss me or not. I made it easy for him. I extended my hand, the one free from my suitcase, and, shaking his, I said, "Thank you for the lift. I'll see you next Saturday."

It was even a little cold for my taste.

Entering a building with the bright-blue door and a sign that read *Kennedy's Bed and Breakfast*, I met a ginger-haired woman who wore her hair closely cropped to her head. She was lovely—slender, freckled, with bright blue eyes. She showed me to my room, which I'd be staying in for the week, and I fell in love with it right away—Irish-lace curtains covered a window that faced a bay. When I shifted the curtain from the window, I looked upon the summer light dancing on the fishing boats at sea.

I unpacked and helped myself to the complimentary tea and biscuit that had been left in the room. After that, I went back to the front desk and asked the host about the address I'd been given at the solicitor's office.

She glanced at it and smiled. "Oh, that's Nora O'Sullivan's place. It's a lovely walk, about two miles. Go left when the road splits by the farm. You'll see a brown mare. When you reach the T in the road, walk straight, then proceed several meters until you see a farmhouse with an oversized weather vane. Then you'll see her driveway. From there, you can almost put your hand into the sea, and you'll be at her house."

I looked at her in stunned silence. This was the age of GPS. The Internet.

"There're no markings on the road. No signs," she said. "But if you want to wait until tomorrow, I'll give you a lift."

Since Fiona, the investigator, hadn't found a working telephone number for Nora and I wanted to try to find her house today, I took it to heart that a walk would do me good.

"Thank you. I think I'll go for a walk and see if I can find it."

The woman gave me an apple. She said it was for the horse I'd see on my walk; she also gave me a treat for a big yellow dog that lived at the same house.

"How do you know I'll see a horse and a dog?"

She laughed. "We just know things here. It's hard to explain. And besides, there's only one road." She brushed her skirt. "I mean no offense. You have family here, and they'll be able to help you understand."

My walk appeared to be preordained. *Am I in some kind of alternate universe where everyone is descended from a long line of psychics? If so, is that why my Aunt Thelma wanted me to travel to the Beara?*

I earnestly felt the need to understand my clairvoyance, which had been activated in a new way since I'd arrived.

I'd followed my host's instructions perfectly, but I felt confused about an hour into my walk, because after I'd gone straight through the T as instructed, I didn't see a horse or a dog and I was walking inland, toward the hills, instead of toward the sea. Finding myself in this situation, I decided to do what I always did, which was give myself a good talking to, since I hadn't gotten a cell phone when I was in Cork and now I was lost.

"Stupid," I said aloud and kicked a stone and watched it skip along the road. At that precise moment, I heard an engine and saw a big, fast-moving van come over the rise. It was in the worst imaginable spot to meet a vehicle, as the dense green underbrush beside the road was as thick as a concrete barrier. I jumped into the greenery anyway as the van veered into the other lane in order to miss me.

The driver, white haired, wasn't fazed. I was the one who didn't know the rules of drivers and pedestrians sharing the road here. I stepped out of my wall of vines and vegetation and picked moss out of my hair. The wrinkled man waved in the distance.

A little bit down the road, I finally saw a brown mare standing at a fence, waiting. I held the apple out to her in the palm of my hand.

"My wild Irish rose," I whispered. She nudged me.

Horses have a huge amount of emotional intelligence.

Up came a yipping yellow dog. I took the treat out of my pocket and gave it to him.

A woman from the farmhouse came down the path toward me and stuck out her hand to shake mine. "Oh, you must be Lizzy. Someone asked if you'd been by yet."

I was relieved. I had feared I would aimlessly wander the Beara for all time and become an Irish legend—a woman who walks the road in a ghostly form. I shivered.

"Cold, are you?" she asked, genuinely concerned.

"A little." I was afraid to admit that I needed directions, or that I was, heaven forbid, lost. "I'm trying to find a relative."

"Who is it that you're looking for?"

"Nora O'Sullivan," I answered.

"Ah," she said. "She said you were coming during the summer solstice. She's waiting for you." The woman brushed her hands together. From the looks of them, she had been working in a garden. "And here you are. All you need to do is go down this road until you see a driveway on the left. Turn there, and it will lead to her house. It's on the right. It sits up proper and faces the sea. That way Nora can see the fairies dance on the hills to the north."

"So it's not far?" I asked.

"Not far at all. And if you get lost in the Beara, concentrate on the answer you need. It comes to you better that way." The woman turned with a gentle wave and headed back toward her house. The horse and dog followed.

I found the gravel driveway that led me to Nora's house. To the right of her home, there lay a path with ceramic mushrooms, and farther away, a cedar pyramid structure.

The door opened before I knocked, and a white-haired woman who looked like Aunt Thelma greeted me. This had to be Nora O'Sullivan.

"Lizzy," she said excitedly. "I've been waiting."

I followed her as she led me into her kitchen. It had a large, round table, covered by a linen tablecloth, something that Aunt Thelma would have cherished. Nora had a pot of tea and a tray of scones sitting out. The tea was hot, like she knew I'd appear when I did. When I saw the pot of tea leaves next to the hot water, I remembered how my Aunt Thelma used to read the leaves. I wondered if Nora did.

"I read tea leaves and stones," she said, reading my mind. "Let me tell you all about it."

I'd just met Nora O'Sullivan, but already I felt at home. And though she resembled my Aunt Thelma, she also looked a little bit like me around her eyes.

"It feels like I've met you before," I said to her, "although I guess that couldn't be true."

Her blue eyes sparkled. They matched the color of the sea today. Green, rolling hills and the dark outline of another peninsula were visible through the window to the north, and I thought I could see seals playing in the bay.

"Oh, we've met before when I was astral traveling."

Over the next hour, Nora told me stories about the fairies she watched from the bay window. I was in a chair facing the ocean, trying to see the fairies too. After a bit, she brought over a ceramic bowl filled with polished stones of every color. Most were the size of pea gravel. She bid me to take off my shoes and dip my bare feet into the bowl of colored gemstones. It felt cool and refreshing, like eating mint-flavored ice cream.

She shook the bowl so my feet plunged farther into the stones— citrine, aquamarine, quartz, amethyst, and others. Then she brought in a tray filled with larger stones, some polished and some rough. She gave me instructions to select six stones at a time. I laid each one out in a vertical row, followed by another six stones in another row, and repeated it until I had selected a total of thirty-six stones.

"I'm able to make predictions and see into the future for six months. Each of the rows of stones on the tray symbolizes a month's time. Today is June twenty-first, so the first row will be from the twenty-first of this month until the same day in July," Nora said.

She brought me paper and pen, and she suggested that I take notes. I scribbled as she talked, enchanted by the ocean, the cozy home setting, and my future for the next six months of my life.

"Ah, you see the first stone that you selected? It means a repair in a relationship with a fella."

I protested. "I've broken up with everyone," I said.

Nora's eyes twinkled at my denial. "Unless you meet someone new in four weeks, you're in repair," she said.

"So soon?" I asked. *It has to be someone new. But if not, who can it be?* The name *Danny* popped into my mind, but I quickly disposed of that impossible idea. *That relationship is over.*

I turned my full attention back toward Nora. "My past relationships with men aren't great, Nora, so I think I'll meet someone new."

She smiled, and her blue eyes twinkled in reply as she went on with the reading. "You picked opal, a semiprecious stone. That means that you are hurt easily. You're also creative in the arts, music, writing, and such."

There's the screenplay I want to write and the new sets for the theaters I plan to design and build.

She continued, "You are to have two new challenges during the period from June to July—exciting, but challenging nonetheless. There's also something about a home or house after a flight. And now we'll move to the period from July twenty-first through August twenty-first," she said. "Dogs and cats love you."

I smiled, thinking of Karma, safe in Manzanita, with my friend.

"Oh," Nora began. She'd picked up the next raw and uncut stone in the second row of the tray and held it for me to see. "And your man is still here."

Gee whiz. Which man is it?

"You picked an unpolished ruby, Lizzy. This stone easily opens a door for you."

She took the next rock between her fingers and held it to the light. "This next stone represents the birth of a new idea; however, there's something to be careful about: a friend or colleague might have a negative response to something. If you listen to that person, you may never do it, so be very careful. Insist that they do not influence you like that."

I squirmed a little at the idea that someone could have such power over me.

49

"There are no obstacles around you," she said, continuing the reading. "And there is something about being overseas."

When I return from Ireland, I need to fix up and sell Thelma's beach house in Manzanita. That was my final job as the executor of her estate.

"From September to October, the tide will turn in your favor." Nora held the stone for me to see. "The old conditions will be gone, and what comes in will be good health, fortune, and everything else—grand events and people right through the front door. You will have love and abundance. Also, a new opportunity will open."

I frantically scribbled to keep up with her, not wanting to break the spell of the moment but yearning for notes so I could remember everything she told me.

"From October to November—you again selected a ruby. Rubies open doors for you. Also, you've selected a raw sapphire."

I looked at it. The sapphire was a dark stone in an unpolished state, and I would never have guessed that it was a precious stone. It didn't sparkle or look like it was special at all.

"It's dim," I said.

"Yes, a dark stone. It means you have high expectations in life that will be fulfilled. But I have to warn you of something else from this time period," she said as she leaned in closer to me. "Be sure to go with your gut feeling, your intuition, because if you don't, things will not go well for you."

That's what Aunt Thelma always told me too.

The final two rows of stones were left. This was bittersweet because I didn't want my stone reading to be over. I'd found a warm cocoon here with Nora.

"God listens to you, and you're not to hide your talent—you are good at what you do."

And with that, we were to the final month, the last six stones. *It's all moving so fast.*

"You will have new things to look forward to in this time. I see some kind of grant or funding ahead for you. And then, another opportunity opens—a contract. And your ambition— never lose sight of it, because you will be able to make money from it. Aim high and you will get it."

After my stone reading, Nora channeled my dead relatives. It felt like everyone in the clan had pulled up a chair at Nora's house.

"In your dreams, your father comes to you, and he is there for you." She laughed as she looked at a vacant chair in the room. "He's a jolly man and wants you to explore your family history on his side while you're in Ireland. He's happy that you're here too."

My relatives are a chorus of spiritual cheerleaders around me.

"Oh, and your great-grandparents and your grandparents are here too; they love you, and they are protecting you."

They love me and are protecting me. Even though I can't remember them.

"And one last thing," Nora said. "Your father tells me that you were his angel on earth."

Chapter 10
The Hag of Beara

AFTER THE STONE READING, NORA gave me a ride back to the bed and breakfast. She asked me to come back to her place for lunch tomorrow. I decided to ask her about the rosary then. I carried it with me all the time now, afraid to leave it anywhere.

I felt sure that Nora would be able to help me find the owner of this rosary through her psychic talents. Aunt Thelma had been able to place her hand over an item and feel vibrations and describe its owner. Word of her talent had brought people from all over the Oregon coast.

I wasn't sure if Nora had the same abilities as my late aunt, but she possessed a talent I'd never seen before with her stone reading. "Each of the stones carries a vibration," she said as she explained how she was able to predict the future. "All this came to me before any books were written about such things," she added.

The bed and breakfast host greeted me after I'd thanked Nora and waved goodbye. I watched her small car turn around and head back toward the sea.

The host glanced out the window and smiled as Nora drove by.

"I see that you found her, just like I said. Supper will be ready in about fifteen minutes."

Going upstairs, I unlocked my door and sighed when everything in my room was as I had left it. I thought about the day so far. I had met Nora and immediately liked her. *I'm so excited!* She was my O'Sullivan family, and a living connection to my Aunt Thelma. Tomorrow I planned to ask Nora how her Catholic beliefs and spiritualism blended in a happy interfaith marriage. *And why not?* The country where fairies and St. Patrick coexisted was a true blend of customs and beliefs.

The bed and breakfast's seafood chowder was orgasmic. It was rich and heady and buttery and filled with the freshest assortment of fish and prawns and scallops. White and red wine were served with it, along with brown bread and butter.

My fellow guests at the B & B—a young couple who had come to bicycle around the Beara and explore Dursey Island—talked about the larger of the two Skellig Islands, Skellig Michael, and said that they'd seen it in the distance while exploring on their bicycles. I'd seen the islands when I was at Mass rock. Liam had told me that monks had lived there in stone beehive huts and kept Christianity alive in the Dark Ages. He added that some people believed that the ghosts of the priests still walked the rock at night.

Dessert was a little meringue nest delicately holding fresh strawberries and topped with a dollop of whipped cream—finished with shaved chocolate sprinkled over it.

After the plates and food were cleared from the table, our host made a suggestion. "Who wants a lift into Castletownbere to hear Luka Bloom sing later tonight?"

"Who's Luka Bloom?" I asked.

"An Irish folk singer. He's the younger brother of Christy Moore."

A musician on the magical Beara in Ireland. *Perfect end to a great day.*

Castletownbere is a small village. Stars sparkled in the black sky as we found a parking place by the sea, not far from the fishing boats moored at the docks. I was mesmerized by the festive lights from the venue reflecting on the water. We were thrilled when we got tickets. So many people milled around outside the entrance, we'd feared it was sold out.

Inside the tiny venue, once a boathouse and now an art gallery, we sat in folding chairs and held our glasses of white wine close to us. It was packed with people. Luka Bloom sang "The City of Chicago." It's a melancholy tale about the Irish who immigrated to Chicago and dreamed of the hills of Donegal. It's the bittersweet story about many Irish who left family behind in Ireland. But many Irish-Americans, like me, return to look for their family connections—their family ties—to better understand themselves.

Chapter 11
Nora's Pyramid

IT RAINED DURING THE NIGHT, and some gusts of wind rattled the B & B, but I tucked myself under my down covers and was quite content. *Actually,* I thought, *this is the most at peace I've been in a long time.*

After a quick shower and a breakfast of porridge, poached eggs, brown-bread toast, and butter, I went back to my room and checked my email with my laptop. I was still giving myself a firm talking to about not having a cell phone in the Beara.

My Uncle Callaghan had emailed about Aunt Thelma's estate and the Irish solicitor. My brother had emailed that Officer John Hall had been to the theater and asked specifically about me.

Nora said that a new man might be coming in my future. I need to concentrate on the present, not the past.

Easier said than done.

After lunch at Nora's house, she invited me into the cedar pyramid, a completely enclosed structure with skylights, crafted of thick, wooden planks. It sat on her property overlooking the sea. I climbed in and discovered a low beach chair where I reclined and inhaled the rich wood scent. Cedar reminded me of Oregon.

"Do you like the pyramid? I noticed you were lost in thought," Nora said as she eased into an identical chair next to mine.

"I was thinking about Oregon, and I was thinking that I've been running away from things, pretty much all my life."

"Anyone inside the pyramid who needs a bit of mending can heal if they want to sit awhile. I don't need to say anything."

I had to agree because I felt a healing energy. "What happens, Nora, when you leave the pyramid? Do you keep the clarity?"

"Ah, that's an insightful question. Most people keep what's learned. Some people don't. It's free will."

"I already feel so connected to Ireland, and especially to the Beara."

"It's your intuition leading you." She gave my hand a little squeeze. "Sit for a while longer, Lizzy. I'll be up at the house when you're ready. Follow the ceramic mushroom stools if you forget your way."

She knows that I get lost easily.

As I sat in the sanctuary of the pyramid, I remembered my last day with Kuruk in Sedona. He'd given me a blessing and sung the travel song to keep me safe. And then I remembered Danny, but I shook that image from my mind. I didn't want to go back to a broken heart.

I'm not good at relationships.

The Hag of Beara sits above Coulagh Bay and has a stunning view of Ballycrovane Harbor. She has lived seven lives. The Cailleach—or the Hag, as she is also called—is a flecked rock that is unlike any other in the Beara.

The Cailleach sits close to Kilcatherine Church, although you can't see the ruins of the church from the Hag. It's only a short walk down a dirt path, and you'll find her. Some believe that if you circle around her three times, from left to right, you can make your wish and it will come true.

She waits with her face turned toward the sea, watching for her husband, Manannán, God of the Sea, to return to her. In one of her lifetimes, she stole a Bible from a priest, so he struck her with a staff and she turned to stone.

"The Cailleach represents the power, fertility, and strength of women in Ireland," Nora said as she dropped me off on the path that led to the Hag. "People bring small tokens and offerings out of respect for her power, and she talks to the strong women on the Beara and to those from other lands if they are willing to listen."

I had told Nora I was curious as to the rosary's ownership, but she and I had decided to tackle it later. She had also offered to read my tea leaves in the afternoon. I fondly remembered that my Aunt Thelma had been able to accomplish just about anything with a good reading of the leaves.

It was a glorious day. The sun was out; I couldn't see a cloud in the sky. Nora drove off and told me she would be back a little later. I was grateful for time alone with the Hag, and there were no other tourists out—at least as far as I could see. The view was lovely, and the sun was warm on my face; I didn't have the anxiety that I'd felt in Cork. I'd whitewashed my meeting with Cormac, and the darkness of the memorial wake, and the ugly words in my pink-flamingo lipstick written on the mirror.

The ancient stone face of the Hag, a woman who represents strength in Ireland, basked in the sun. I looked at the euros left in her nooks and crevices; someone had even left a brightly colored scarf—greens with flecks of pink and orange—wrapped around her as a fashionable gift.

Bits of bone, wood, and shell—all natural treasures—also covered her. I thought about how she looked out at the bay and waited for the god of the sea to return to her after all these years. There was a light breeze that made the grass around the Hag ripple.

I closed my eyes and breathed in the fresh air and had a sense of calm and balance that all was aligned in the world. When I opened my eyes, I was surprised to see a young woman in her early twenties walking down the path toward the Hag. She had copper-colored hair and came with a gift of almsgiving. She nodded to greet me. Walking around the Hag three times, she put a ribbon from her hair on the flecked stone and placed her hand on it.

I went to sit on a sparse piece of grass a little bit in the distance. I wanted to give the young woman the time she needed with the Hag. Luckily, it was dry enough to sit down. I looked at the ocean with a yearning toward home. My life felt adrift. *What's after this? Aunt Thelma's beach house to fix up, mend, and sell, but what then?*

I looked over to see if my visitor was still with the Hag. She was, but she'd turned away from me. I stood up and took some coins out of my pocket. I wanted to leave something for the Cailleach. I was ready to walk around it three times the way the young woman had, but when she turned back toward me, I jumped back in fright: I saw the aged face of a woman with a veil of black granite staring at me. The woman turned away quickly, and when she turned back toward me again, she had the youthful face of the woman I'd first seen.

"It looks like a ghost you've seen," she said to me.

"I'm sorry," I said, both embarrassed and tongue-tied.

"Don't apologize," she interrupted. "If it's an old woman's face, it was the Hag herself. She's been known to do that."

Chapter 12
Reading the Tea Leaves

"You're lucky the Cailleach visited you."

Nora and I were sitting at her kitchen table, drinking tea. The view of the ocean was mesmerizing. Today the Atlantic looked more blue than gray.

"Although, sometimes she isn't nice," Nora added. "You've asked me for a bit of advice about a rosary?"

I nodded as I sipped the tea and admired the view.

"Drink your tea, and I'll read the leaves."

Aunt Thelma could extract detailed predictions from tea leaves, about one to twenty-four hours in the future. When I was young, I found it annoying when she would predict my day like she was reading a horoscope. While I was going through the angst of junior high and high school, it seemed like a cheap parlor trick—except she was always so accurate.

"What do you know about reading tea leaves?" Nora asked as I finished my tea and left about a half a teaspoon of liquid at the bottom.

"My aunt always told me that tea from China was the best for telling your fortune. She said that it was purer than the tea she got from India. Too much dust and chaff in the Indian tea."

I was down to the prerequisite half a teaspoon and handed my cup over to Nora. It was a traditional teacup shape—which I knew also gave a clearer image in the bottom of the cup than a mug. Taking it from me, Nora twirled it around three times from left to right, and then she expertly removed the excess liquid by pouring it into the saucer. Looking at the tea leaves that remained in my cup, she began by telling me some history.

"It was the Scottish Highlander peasants who began the practice of reading the tea leaves. It's believed that if a tea reader takes money for the service, the reading will be swayed by the coin. That's why most tea readers will not take money for the service."

I remembered that my Aunt Thelma would never take any money for her readings. Sometimes, though, I would wake up and find a nice pile of seasoned wood for our fireplace on the porch or a basket of fruit. People found a way to thank her.

"The rim represents your nearest future," Nora said. "The sides of the cup symbolize the not-so-distant future, and the bottom is farther out in time. Even though the reading only extends about twenty-four hours into the future, sometimes I can predict even later events to come. This is because one event leads to the next, and of course, leads to the next. There are no coincidences. There is no chance."

I remember this from Aunt Thelma. The information was remote because I'd pushed it back into the recesses of my mind, but it was still there. Nora was helping me remember.

"You have the symbol of the crescent moon and circles on the rim. This means joy is in your heart." She looked down the sides of the teacup. "And your leaves are pressed in a circular pattern on the sides. That means happiness."

Nora stopped midsentence as she pondered my farthest future. She didn't say anything for a long time. Finally, she looked at me with her blue eyes sparkling. "Lizzy, I must give you the truth in the reading—even if it's not good news."

I remembered that about Thelma too. She could predict a breakup with a current boyfriend or a bad grade on a test that I'd take later in the day. When I was younger, I didn't want to know. Now I regretted the missed opportunity to learn from her.

"It's all coming back to me—how my aunt would read my tea leaves, and I didn't appreciate it. But now it's different. I want the truth, and I want to know."

Nora sighed deeply. "Your farthest future leaves are in the shape of a cross. It's a dark omen. There are small pistols within the bottom of the cup—a double omen. You need to be alert to minimize or avert the danger."

"I'm in danger now. Maybe not currently, but before. It's been that way since Cork."

"You'll live through it. I can see your future beyond, but make no mistake, it will be a trial. And you'll find something you've been seeking all your life in the north, in the city of Belfast."

Belfast? I wondered what could be there.

"In Belfast your past and future combine. If you ever feel lost or confused, remember, that's where you need to go. Now," she said, "I need a nap." She excused herself from the table, looking a little older.

The remnants of my tea leaves remained in the cup. I inspected the tiny flecks of tea. I didn't see any of the things Nora saw, but I knew she spoke the truth. A line from *Macbeth* came to me: *Double, double toil and trouble. Fire burn, and cauldron bubble!*

I spent about an hour in the pyramid. Walking back to the house, I found that Nora was up and about. She had a fresh pot of tea and a tray of warm scones ready.

I took out the antique rosary and placed it on the table between us.

Nora picked it up and held it in her hand. "Wooden beads and one rough stone, with a ring on the end."

"Can you tell me the owner? Thelma could sometimes get a sense of the owner of an object. Even the briefest of descriptions could help."

She set the rosary on the table and hovered her hand over the top of it. "I see black night without any stars—and something hidden. A cave or maybe a tunnel perhaps." She shook her head. "I'm sorry, but I'm not getting anything else. Ownership of items isn't my specialty."

"You're not able to see anyone?" Secretly, I was disappointed.

Nora left the room for a minute, and when she came back, she was carrying letters. They were on fancy stationery, the kind my Aunt Thelma adored. "O'Sullivan psychics are gifted. Thelma was talented, and so was your mother, even though you didn't know her."

She handed one of Aunt Thelma's letters to me. "She wrote me when she adopted you after your mother left, and she wrote when your father died. Lizzy, she wanted you to embrace your talent as a psychic."

Why haven't I believed in myself?

Because I didn't want to be different; I didn't want friends to whisper about my crazy aunt and my family. I'd worked hard to fit in and wear the same clothes—though we couldn't afford it, my aunt had found a way to make me feel like my friends. Now I regretted that I'd lost the chance to be different. I'd missed the opportunity to learn from her.

It's not too late. Nora can teach me.

In our sessions together, I found my psychic talents were strongest regarding *psychometry*, the feel of an object, and *precognition*, in the way I sensed danger. Sometimes miniature movie clips flashed in front of me when I hovered my hand over an object or when I touched it. After hours in Nora's kitchen, attempting to see the fairies making forts on the cliffs (Nora could always see them), and working with the tea leaves and stones with people from the village, I knew I had gained as much as I could from Nora. It was time for me to have faith in my abilities. My time in the Beara was over now, and I was restless to go.

Chapter 13
Stone Circle

LIAM'S CAR ROLLED UP AND parked in front of the bed and breakfast in the early morning. He was right on time. I was sitting on a bench in front of the inn, savoring a delicious cup of coffee.

I'd walked to the tiny post office in Eyeries earlier that morning. I bought a mailing envelope and packing supplies and gently wrapped the rosary. At the counter, I handed it to a woman, who weighed it, affixed the postage to the USA, and put it in a bag for delivery. Then I'd walked back to the bed and breakfast and checked out—after thanking my host for all the hospitality.

"Enjoy the scenery in the Beara?" Liam's aura was a deep shade of pink. *Lust.* I blushed and turned my face toward the sun.

"Yes," I said. "I found what I needed."

"Want to see a stone circle?"

In the middle of a farmer's field, I dodged cow piles as Liam and I walked along a grassy path toward an ancient stone circle. Its center was a flat stone, small like a paver in a pathway. Lined around the center stone, upright, were twelve vertical stones, each of them between three and seven feet tall: Derreenataggart Stone Circle.

"It's believed that this stone circle originally had fifteen stones," Liam said as we walked around the inside of the circle. I touched each stone. The circle reminded me of the medicine wheel I'd seen, a different type of stone circle, in Sedona. It made me realize that stone circles transcend cultures.

"In Ireland, historians believe that stone circles were constructed for ceremonial and ritual purposes. The two tallest stones usually mark the entrance to the stone circle from the northeast side. The axial stone, set directly opposite the entrance, is usually the shortest. There are more than a hundred stone circles in Ireland that contain from five to fifteen stones—always an uneven number. When diagrammed, the stone circle in some way aligns with something significant in the stars."

I wanted to feel some of the vibrations that I'd felt in the vortex I'd visited in Arizona. I remembered the tingling sensation that began at my feet and traveled all the way up into my core. Here, however, I didn't feel anything, which surprised me. *Maybe 3,000 years make psychometric observations difficult. Or perhaps I'm not really psychic,* I thought, allowing self-doubt to creep inside. I pushed it away and walked to the next stone.

While I had my palm flat on the westernmost-facing stone, I began to hear whispers like the ones I had from the Ogham stones in the hall at University College Cork, so I closed my eyes and listened. I hoped this wasn't a psychotic episode—stones whispering to me?

Nora believes in me. I have to believe in me.

I stepped toward another lichen-covered stone. Cloud shapes appeared, quickly changing in the wind. A breeze came, and the grass around the stones fluttered. Somehow, time was getting thinner and thinner inside the stone circle. I couldn't explain it, but I didn't push it away. Instead, I placed some coins for good luck under the center flat stone of the stone circle.

Something has changed for me.

The lift to Cork seemed uneventful until I heard an engine behind us. I turned around and heard a ping. When I turned back, I watched in shocked horror as the windshield burst into a kaleidoscope of broken glass. An echo of a bullet over my left ear exploded as more glass flew over us.

I remembered the warning Nora had given me with the tea-leaf reading. I just hadn't expected the danger to arrive so soon. "Who's shooting at us?" I yelled at Liam as the wind howled through the giant hole in the front of the car.

We were careening around curves at a terrifying rate. For a minute, I flashed back to my time in Arizona, just before I plunged over a red-rock, desert cliff.

Liam pushed a gun into my hand. I hadn't known that he had one. "It's loaded," he yelled. "Do you know how to use it?"

I turned around and pointed the gun at the car whose driver was firing at us. I squeezed the trigger.

My husband had taught me. One birthday, he surprised me with a target range lesson. I didn't enjoy it, the day I learned how to shoot, but now I was thankful for the little bit that I'd learned. I pulled the trigger, over and over. I didn't count the number of shots, but I unloaded everything in the chamber. The pursuing car lost ground and began to fall behind on the road. White and gray smoke billowed from it. I turned back to our shattered windshield as Liam sped up to put more distance between us and the shooters.

"I think we've lost them," I said. He glanced behind us and shifted down to a lower gear.

Liam took the now-empty gun from my hands and stuffed it under his bucket seat while he kept his eyes on the road ahead.

Who keeps a gun in his car—in Ireland? A man with secrets.

At my dorm room door, I'd looked forward to changing my clothes and picking out the slivers of glass still in my hair. That hope was lost when Liam and I saw the note on my dorm room door; he gave it to me. It was from Aidan. He'd written that Inspector Keating had been to the room and made another report.

Inside the room, the mattress had been cut open and its stuffing had fallen on the floor like snow. What was left of the mattress looked like a gutted deer. Liam stepped over stuffing and an overturned chair. I looked at what was left of my room and knew it was time for answers. "What do you know about Cormac's double life?"

Liam flinched as he righted the chair. "Best leave it to the gardaí."

That's not the way it works. At least not for me.

"I don't like cops. I have reasons for that, and I'm not leaving it to them. This gutted mattress is a metaphor for me. Inspector Keating told me to stay out of the Troubles, but I'm involved. Tell me what you know. My life depends on it."

Liam took my hand and led us to a quiet pub near the campus. When the copper-haired waitress came over, I ordered the seafood chowder, brown bread, and a pint of Guinness. If I was going to die, it wasn't going to be without at least one pint in my gut—and some food.

"Tell me what you know," I insisted. "And don't leave anything out. Since my *chance* meeting with Cormac, I have been threatened in Irish with my bright-pink lipstick, I witnessed your brother attacked by a knife-wielding man, and I was almost killed today." I stopped as the waitress set down two perfect-headed pints in front of us. As soon as she was out of sight I added in a whisper, "I need to know!"

Liam looked resigned. While I waited for him to respond, I spooned the butter-rich, creamy broth of the fish chowder to my lips. *Ah. Paradise is an excellent bowl of seafood chowder in Ireland.* I'd found something about the Irish rain and saltwater air, combined with the fresh fish, that made this marriage of chowder with Guinness and brown bread and butter sinful. *Venial,* I thought. *And I still need to get to confession, or maybe not?* I was conflicted in my spiritual beliefs. *Catholic or spiritualist? What's my personal truth?*

Liam took a bite of his sandwich. "Cormac was the youngest in the family and spoiled." He stopped his narrative when the waitress wiped down a table next to us. When she was gone, he continued. "He was charming and reckless. His political leanings were passionate. I hoped his church vocation would save him."

"Was he raising money to usurp the peace?" I whispered. "To bring back the Troubles?"

Liam rubbed his hand through his hair in dismay. "Jesus, Mary, and Joseph. All I know is there are people who wanted him dead."

"So, who was that *blow-in* in mass?"

Liam's attention had turned toward the bar, and the pub had grown quiet. Before, there had been an easy chatter to cover our whispered conversation.

I looked over at two men, dressed all in black, standing at the bar, who were staring at us. I took a deep breath and whispered to Liam, "I hope we can find some help."

Chapter 14
The Plot Thickens

I WAS SURPRISED THAT WE weren't followed when we left the pub. Liam brought us to a mustard-colored house with maroon trim. Michael answered the door and quickly ushered us inside, looking behind us to make sure that no one had followed. "It's even worse than I imagined," he said.

We all entered the kitchen, and had only been there a minute when a catastrophic crash came from the front of the house. Liam, Michael, and I ran from the kitchen into the living room to see what it was, and then they prostrated themselves on the floor like priests at an altar. I wasn't so fast or so smart about drive-by shootings.

"Get down!" Liam screamed at me.

I didn't register it quickly enough. A quick succession of *pop, pop, pop* rang through the air, followed by the squeal of tires on pavement. The next thing I knew, my white blouse was turning red.

Blood. Mine.

Liam rushed me out of Michael's house toward a car parked in the back. "Hospital," I croaked as the red spot on my white shirt grew larger.

And then a *buzz* started in my head, and I drifted away.

I wasn't with Liam and Michael—rather, I was in the Arizona sun with Danny. We were standing by a manzanita bush, and he'd snapped off a piece of one of its branches. His raven hair rustled in the wind.

Why am I in the desert?

I was ready to ask that question when Danny put his mouth to my lips and kissed me. He smelled of fresh manzanita and pinion pine. All parts of my body tingled with heat. Kuruk, the elderly Navajo medicine man, stepped forward. He held his staff, which was embedded with uncut diamonds. He looked at my blood.

"It's not her time," Kuruk said, urgent.

"I'll guide her back," Danny offered.

But I want to stay in the desert with you. It's warm, and I don't hurt.

A light sparkled in the gray-black sky, and transfixed, I stared at it. I wanted to say something else to Kuruk and Danny, but they had disappeared. Then I groaned as the light in the sky changed to the dome light in Michael's car.

"Go away," I growled. *I want to go back to the desert.*

A new voice spoke that was rich and deep. I turned my head and viewed a man in the brown robes of a Franciscan brother. He looked like Saint Francis of Assisi. Or at least he looked like the statuary I'd seen of Saint Francis.

"*Sláinte,*" he said. "I'll tend to that wound." He rolled me to my good side and removed a blood-soaked towel. I felt woozy and winced in pain.

"Bullet went straight through, more like a graze, an open furrow, but she's lost a lot of blood. I'll put in stitches, give her a shot of antibiotics, treat for shock, and then with rest and some rich broth, she should be better in a few days."

The first jab of the needle made me gasp, but when he was finished, and I had been given something for pain, I slipped into a difficult sleep. I dreamed about the men we'd seen in the pub, drinking. But whatever the Franciscan had given me was strong, and the dream faded, gone for good.

I woke by a peat fire that warmed the room. I swung my feet over the edge of a twin bed. My arm was bound in a sling. I willed my legs to make me stand after shoving the blankets to one side with my good arm.

So far so good.

A shadow appeared in the open door. It was the Franciscan.

"My name is Brother O'Mahony," he said. "Good that you're awake. I'll fetch you some bone-marrow broth." The brown robes of the Franciscan disappeared through the door.

The outside loomed with green hills and a few white specks—sheep? But not another house around—at least that I could see.

I heard Brother O'Mahony's footsteps again; he came out with a mug of steaming broth. "It's hot," he cautioned me about the handle of the mug. Sipping the rich soup with hints of onion and garlic, I felt better.

"Where'd you learn to be a doctor?" I asked.

"I'm a veterinarian. I spend more time with animals than human souls. I took my time and made the stitches small and fine. You won't be having much of a scar."

"Where are Liam and Michael, and where am I?" I asked.

"Once they knew you were tended to, they left. I told them I'd have you as good as new within a few days. And you're in County Cork."

I vaguely remembered taking care of my bodily needs, but other than that, time was a blur. The pills that Brother O'Mahony had given me seemed large enough for sheep, and now I realized they probably were. "How long have I been here?" I asked.

"Three days," he said and looked out the open door toward the horizon. "I'd be expecting Liam back soon."

Brother O'Mahony encouraged me to drink more broth. "I'll be letting you have a little more rest now, but if you're feeling up to it, there's a hot shower over there," he said. The brown-robed priest nodded in the direction of a stone outbuilding. "Make yourself comfortable."

The smell of lanolin from the sheep wafted through the morning air.

"It's none of my business, as I tend to the sheep and a garden," he said, waving his hand across the expanse of green, rolling hills, "but you should know that you've been talking in your sleep. You've called out a name for the past three days."

Blankets swaddled me close, like a child in the womb. "Whose name did I call?" I felt a blush grow from my neck to the tops of my cheeks.

"Danny," Brother O'Mahony whispered. He slipped from the room and left me with my thoughts.

Chapter 15
Moving On

I WASN'T FEELING HOLY AS I readied myself to leave the safety of Brother O'Mahony. Looking at Liam over the *boot* (the trunk) of the car, I sucked in air. His resemblance to Cormac was striking; with the wind blowing his hair, and his dark eyes, he was exceedingly handsome. I was unwilling to succumb to an analysis of my failed relationships; therefore, my current emotional state had me confused. I swung into the car seat, and Liam bent to buckle my seat belt. *Oh God, he even smells like Cormac.* His spicy scent spilled over me, and I suppressed a groan. I'd been cooped up in the stone cottage with Brother O'Mahony for too long. I wasn't destined for a nunnery. I felt all parts of my body tingle as Liam sat next to me in the driver's seat. I'd just accepted my penance from Father O'Mahony, having given him my holy confession—no matter where my spiritual beliefs were headed, it felt like a prudent act of faith to hedge my bets.

You haven't sinned again yet.

Sensing my discomfort, Liam asked, "Do you need something?" And before I could answer he added, "Would you like some music?"

I wiggled in the bucket seat. "Sure," I answered about the music. "Where's Michael?"

"Belfast," he answered. "We'll be needing some help there. We'll be joining him."

Lush greenery rushed past us as I gazed out the window. White spots of sheep grazed in the distant hills. I rubbed the crease between my eyebrows. *As soon as we check into the hotel, I will, one, take a frigid shower to freeze my hormones, and two—hell, I don't know.* The pain from my arm overcame all the reasoning powers I had left in me.

"Fine," I said sharply.

Belfast. *Nora's prediction.*

We checked into the Jury Inn in Belfast. Our rooms were side by side, because I insisted on it. I wasn't sure how I felt about Liam. Chemistry was there, but it was all complicated by the events that had proceeded it.

We were in an older section of the hotel, connected to the lobby through an underground walkway. The halls were dark as night, but automatic sensors illuminated our path as we found our separate rooms. Liam pointed out two emergency-exit doors that fed into alleys. Using plastic door keys, we had an awkward goodnight as he gave me a hug—I knew he wanted more from me physically, but I was conflicted about what I wanted. I decided to do nothing until I had sorted out my feelings.

I pressed my back against the door after I'd locked it. I hurt.

Hormonal headache. I need a cold shower. Stepping inside the bathroom, I sighed. *A tub. A real, honest to goodness, I-can-soak-myself tub.* I filled the bathtub with hot water and eased my tired body—except for my arm—into the water. The soap from the hotel was scented, a lavender-therapy spa brand. Luxuriating, I ruminated on everything that had occurred since the moment I deplaned in Cork.

My skin was wrinkling from the long soak in the water. I finally pulled the bathtub plug and watched the water go down the drain. Maybe I should have taken a cab to the airport, but then I thought about Nora's prediction: my past and future would come together in Belfast.

A sharp siren from the hotel's fire alarm broke my chain of thought. *I'm naked. Please stop that screaming siren.*

It didn't listen. The high-pitched frenzy of the siren continued. Only half dressed, in my Victoria Secret bra and heart undies, I heard a knock on the door.

"Hotel security. Evacuate now!"

My T-shirt was twisted over my head, caught on my sling. I grabbed my passport and Visa card and stuffed each one in my bra. I reached for my bag with my laptop. I ran to the door, unlocked it, stepped into the hallway—which was dark, except for the strobe light of the alarm—and ran into a brick wall in the form of a muscled man, dressed all in black, whose face was covered in a balaclava. A moment later, I realized that there were two other men with him.

There wasn't smoke, and I had a feeling there wasn't a fire. And I knew I wasn't facing hotel security. The metallic taste surged in my throat, and all the hairs on my arms stood straight up in a salute. The large muscled man farthest to the right side picked me up like I was a feather duster and threw me over his shoulder.

"Hey, my arm hurts!"

I hit him with my other one, but he was built like one of Ireland's stone walls. The three men didn't listen to me. I felt stuck, like a fly in a sticky trap. So I screamed. The noise of the fire alarm and the dark hallway made it easy for the men to exit through the alleyway with no one else around to hear me. *Why am I wriggling like a worm from the shoulder of a balaclava-clad man? And where is Liam?*

This was the land of green, rolling hills, saints, and shamrocks. It was also the land of the Troubles. And I'd stepped in a pile of it.

"Hey," I hissed at the man who had me over his shoulder, "there must be a mistake. Go find yourself a princess to kidnap."

All I heard was Irish, and I didn't understand any of it. *Where is everyone else? Is this wing vacant? Where is the hotel staff?*

"Leave me alone!" I yelled as I hit my assailant with my healthy arm. A hood was slipped over my head, and it smelled like piss. I suppressed a gag as sweat trickled down my back.

I was pushed into a van. At least I figured it was a van, because of the way the door sounded as it slid closed. Things were going from bad to worse. Once in a vehicle, I knew, a kidnap victim's chances of survival diminish. I hoped mine had not been extinguished. I couldn't see anything through the black hood—the eye slits were sewed shut.

"I'm thirsty," I complained. "And my arm hurts."

Someone thumped me on the head. "Still thirsty," I complained again.

That's when I smelled a chemical scent that I remembered from biology class. Ether.

Oh dear.

A rag was pushed under my hood and held to my nose. I struggled and kicked, but I heard a pulsating sound that vibrated in my head and my ears rang with a loud *buzz, buzz, buzz.*

Even though I struggled, the chemical won. And this time, I didn't dream about anyone.

When I came back to consciousness, the vehicle had stopped. Even though I was still hooded, I struggled and kicked like my life depended on it.

I heard the sound of the ocean crashing against rocks. My balaclava was finally lifted, and what I saw confirmed what I had heard—the sea was breaking against cliffs nearby. It was such a desolate location; I feared the worst. *No one will ever find me. One push over the cliff and it's over.*

I screamed, but the sound was lost over the roar of the ocean. One of the hooded men pulled me toward the edge as I kicked and yelled. I pushed down bile. I'd always feared heights.

Is it possible to survive if I hit water?

Masked again, I was spun around again and then let go. I didn't dare take a step because I didn't know which way to go. Sweat ran down my back. *Maybe they aren't going to toss me over the edge of the cliff. Maybe they'll put a bullet in my head and toss me in a bog. Either way, I'll never be found.*

I'd been told by Aidan that the devil controlled the hearts of some Irish. When fishing couldn't support the family, men stopped trolling for seafood and cast nets for drugs instead. Fishing boats were the favored means by which to import heroin and cocaine. From the boats it made its way to villages, petrol stations, and pubs. I feared that drugs were involved with the events that were in motion here. Perhaps I'd stumbled into a kind of criminal drama that afflicts dealers, addicts, and desperate people who medicate with drugs.

Clank! I heard a lock click like a final explanation point. It was dank and musty smelling. I took the black balaclava from my head, and my arm ached with pain. Looking around, I saw that I was in an underground room. It was full of shadows. Some kind of underground storage area. It looked to have provisions for some time. Shelves held supplies—dried food, matches, protein bars, freeze-dried food packages, and bottles of Irish whiskey.

Kidnappers left me locked in a hole. How long will it take me to tunnel out of this underground grave?

I took out a sealed bottle of Jameson's whiskey from a wooden shelf. I blew dust off the top of the bottle and inspected the label. *Sine Metu.* It was the motto of Jameson's, meaning without fear. My brother had told me what it meant, after a toast to my health on a birthday, in what felt like a long time ago. There were two more bottles of the top-of-the-line, 100-proof, single-cask Jameson's whiskey sitting on the shelf.

There was a cot with a blanket and pillow. *Why did I open that door in the hotel?* I opened the whiskey and slouched on the cot.

Are these supplies for fishing boats? Or smuggling something else? Looking down at the bottle, I found it was half empty. *Or half full,* I thought with bitter irony. Either way, my head was spinning like a dreidel. *Drunk.*

I closed one eye to stop the spinning.

I've often wondered if dreams belong to the spirit world, where angels and enlightened beings find a way to deliver messages, or if it is the subconscious that works to problem-solve during slumber. Maybe it is both. I woke with a start, and for a moment, I'd lost all sense of time. *How long has it been since I was kidnapped? What do they want? Will anyone find me?*

I hadn't found anything with which to dig my way out, like a shovel, but I had found a fork, and I thought that was at least the beginning of a plan. Crawling, I crept back toward the entrance of my underground prison. Using my hand as a guide, I felt the cool earth.

I didn't know whether it was night or day.

In my dream, I found a way to open the door. In the way of dreams, it was scattered and pieced together like a quilt. Claustrophobia and anxiety were my constant companions. I had no water. Being buried alive was taking a toll on me. The words at Cormac's wake, about the woman buried alive in her coffin, filled me with dread.

At the door, I found a metal latch, cold and hard. It didn't budge. I pounded on the door in frustration, over and over. Finally, I collapsed in a ball on the cool ground.

Now I remember. When I felt like this before.

Rebecca Fuller, the *Sedona Red Rock News* reporter, had been taken by force into a Navajo mine, and she had survived. I'd found dynamite in there. I wasn't as lucky this time. I thought about what I did have: A fork. Matches. Alcohol.

I was ready to try the door again, but I heard something, or someone, outside. Frightened, I scrambled away from the door, along the tunnel, back to the main room.

The air was fresher here than it had been by the door. *How am I getting outside air?*

I was positive that I heard someone at the entrance. Then I heard the door shut and heavy footsteps coming toward me. Only one of the balaclava-hooded men entered the main room this time, but someone else was with him. That person had a white pillowcase over his or her head.

The white pillowcase was removed, and I stared in shock. "*Cormac,*" I gasped.

Like Lazarus, raised from the dead.

Chapter 16

Escape

I WASN'T GOING TO SPEND another minute underground—at least alive—if I had anything to do with it. And while part of me wanted to learn the details about Cormac's return from the dead, the rosary, and his part in the dramatic events that had turned my life upside down, my desire for survival was stronger.

I'm not going to stay in this godforsaken grave any longer. I had the fork, I had the alcohol, and I had the matches. And I'd had a lot of time to think about it. No time to change plans; this was my opportunity, and I was going to take it. Without hesitating, I withdrew the metal fork from my bra. The kidnapper was close enough to me—my opportunity had materialized; I stabbed the man in black with the fork tines on the top of his hand as hard as I could. Then I twisted it.

I was quick and effective. My kidnapper was still on his feet, but I jammed my knee into his crotch—he grabbed his testicles, gasped for air, and fell into the fetal position.

It wasn't over yet. I lit a match. Touching the end of a linen rag that I'd shoved into a bottle filled with Jameson's, I put a light to the end of it.

Cormac had duct tape over his mouth, but his legs were un-bound. I tossed the bottle into a corner, respecting the special high-proof alcohol for its ability to burn (though I was feeling some remorse that such fine drink wasn't going to be consumed); it broke and exploded in fire with a *whoosh* sound. I yelled to Cormac, "Run!" I stumbled through the tunnel toward the door. If it was locked from the outside, I knew this was a bad decision. *Life or death. I hope it's life.*

My escape came to me in a dream. That's how I'd devised my plan. Whether it was angels and saints as divine messengers or just my subconscious, I don't know. But after waking from a vivid dream, I'd known I had to start a fire, and it didn't matter that Cormac was with me now.

When I reached the door, it yielded, and I pushed my way out into the inky darkness of night. A slight moon provided enough light that I could see the cliffs. *Not that way.*

I thought I heard someone behind me, but I didn't wait.

Run now!

A single misstep and I could break my leg—or worse yet, some-one might grab me again. Or kill me.

A sliver of moon was all I had to navigate by in the dark night. I was an animal fleeing from a hunter.

I need to get as far away as fast as I can. Gripped in panic, I ran over fields, jumped over stone fences, and tried to maintain some hope that I could stay alive.

Chapter 17
Farmhouse Frenzy

SCRAMBLING OVER ROCK AND TURF, I felt a pang of remorse about Cormac. Had he escaped?

My primal urge to survive was stronger than my need to know. I'd gone quite a distance before I slowed down to catch my breath. That's when I saw a dot of light, perhaps from a window? When I squinted I could make out the image of a stone cottage with more dots of light—more windows.

I knew it was most likely after midnight since it didn't really get dark in Ireland at this time of year until about then. Or maybe it was some early hour of the morning before the sun rose again.

I started to formulate a post-escape plan. I'd looked over my shoulder for a long time, but no one had followed me.

What story should I use if I find someone awake at the cottage?

Not that I was kidnapped and held hostage.

As I reached the cottage, I'd decided on my tale. In the past, I'd had arguments and fights with my husband, and I knew that this would sound closer to the truth than what had really occurred. Of course, thinking of him reminded me of his cheating ways. *I'm glad I don't have to deal with him anymore.*

I heard the growl of a dog. *Great. Angry dog.*

A lace curtain was pulled back, and I looked into the dark eyes of a farmer. The dog, I discovered, was a border collie. It jumped up beside him to get a better view of me.

Maybe it only wants to herd me, not hurt me.

The farmer didn't open the door at first. I wasn't sure that I would have opened the door for me either. I must have looked a fright. Nevertheless, after a few moments had passed, he opened it to face me. I sucked in a breath, took a page from my real past life, and told a lie with enough conviction that I could see his face begin to soften.

"My husband and I had an argument. Out on the highway; I had to run away." I said it all as breathlessly as I could, which wasn't difficult since I was still short-winded from running away.

I heard a female voice. *Maybe his wife?*

She walked over with a shotgun in her hands. *Maybe this isn't such a good idea.*

I was ready to turn and leave. "Come on inside. The wife knows what you'd be talking about." Then he quickly added, "But not because of the likes of me."

My poker face in full play, I drew a story from the time my husband and I were at the end of our relationship. I'd walked in on him having sex with a woman with enormous boobs. Though his revolver had been right there on the nightstand, I didn't shoot either one of them—although I was tempted—and as it turned out, she was one of many.

"I only told him we should call for help," I said, well into my imaginary story about how the car had broken down—a long way away from here—and that I'd run away from my husband because I was in fear of him.

The wife had brought out steaming cups of herbal tea and Digestives, a delicious cookie-type wafer.

"He was ready to hit me." I allowed the rims of my eyes to get red from some tears. Every word out of my mouth was close to the truth, except what I was describing had been in another place and time.

As I wove the tale in the farmhouse, the peat fire gave off warmth, and the tea and Digestives made the emptiness in my stomach subside. I was getting sleepy with food and fire. From the mantle clock, I discovered that it was now the early hours of the morning. At some point I'd either be offered a place to sleep or would have to leave. When I'd finished my story, I still didn't have an offer. So I thanked my hosts for their hospitality and got up to leave. The dog stood and escorted me to the door.

I caught the brief look between the farmer and his wife—the kind that comes from years of marriage, communication without words—and the old man sighed deeply. "Well, why don't you wait until the morning light? We can offer some porridge and honey before you set off."

"And I'm headed into town tomorrow, so I can give you a lift," the farmer's wife added.

I happily accepted the offer. She guided me to a tiny bedroom in the back of the house and left me alone, and I breathed a sigh of relief. Since I was exhausted, I was sure I'd be asleep in minutes. But, all of a sudden, I knew something was wrong. Then I heard it. Through the walls there was a whispered exchange between the farmer and his wife. I overheard that he planned to call the gardaí—right now.

Yikes! I sat up when I heard her capitulate.

I unlocked the window and slipped outside with my shoes in my hand, my bare feet registering the cool ground. I sprinted away from the house, hopped over a stone fence, and ran away. My heart hammered in my throat as I reached into my bra, cupping my passport and Visa.

Run!

Chapter 18
Finding a Train

IT WAS DARK AS I fled over fields and stone fences. Finally, I had to sit down to catch my breath. While I did so, I watched as green hills exploded with light at the morning's sunrise.

When I got to a road, I followed it into a town—probably the one that the farmer and his wife had spoken about. I felt lucky; it had a small store, and it was open.

The storekeeper cast an uneasy glance at me when I walked in. I was a long way off the tourist path, and I had to look and smell awful from my sweat and the reek of the whiskey, not to mention my sour clothes and unwashed body. *I'm a stinky blow-in with an American accent.*

Looking around the small grocery section of the store, I gathered some fresh fruit, candy bars, packages of nuts, and a cup of hot coffee and brought them to the cash register.

"Is there a way I could get a lift to Belfast?" I handed the cashier my Visa.

She hesitated. When she gave me back my credit card, she finally said, "If it was me, I'd take the train."

"There's a train station nearby?"

"A block down and on your right."

The train station ticket sales booth was manned by a fellow who liked to flirt. He was old and tattered, and he must not have had a very good sense of smell. Or maybe he couldn't smell me because I was on the opposite side of the glass partition.

"When is the next train to Belfast?" I asked.

"It'll leave in about an hour," he said. "Unless," he added, "you want to take a later train, and I'll meet you in an hour over there for a pint." He nodded to a tiny pub across the street and smiled.

"One ticket, please, for the train leaving in an hour." I slid my Visa through the slit in the glass that separated us.

"A one-way ticket, then?" His gray, bushy eyebrows shot up to the middle of his forehead, and his mouth curled in a frown.

Oh, the Irish.

"Yes, thank you, please."

Luckily for me, the train was on time, so I didn't have to side step the ticket man, who kept looking at me. I'd had enough from men for a while.

On the train, a woman came along with a cart of coffee, juice, sandwiches, and candy. I bought coffee and a chicken sandwich, plus a candy bar. I planned to save the chocolate for later.

My goal was to stay in Belfast for at least a day. I planned to collect myself and see if any psychic signs came to me that I should stay in Belfast for more than a night. I remembered Nora's prediction: "In Belfast your past and future combine. If you ever feel lost or confused, remember, that's where you need to go."

At the Belfast station, I wove through the crowd in the railroad terminal and followed the signs to find a taxi. There wasn't much of a line at the taxi stand.

"Can you recommend a hotel?" I asked my driver. He had black, short-trimmed hair and wore chunky silver jewelry on his large-knuckled fingers.

He took me to a hotel on College Street, less than a block from the Grand Opera House. "The Opera House has the distinction of being one of the most bombed buildings in the city's history," he said. "Not to worry," he added, "there's a peace agreement now."

He babbled about the great bonfires starting soon, like a little boy talking about parades, and how the fires would smolder for at least a week.

"Oh, it's a grand time to be visiting Belfast," he said.

Chapter 19
Murals and Past Troubles

SAFELY CHECKED IN TO A different hotel, I took a shower and used the courtesy blow-dryer in the room to dry my hair. I was grateful for hot water and electricity. Clean and in my new clothes that I'd bought in a next-door boutique, I went to the lobby and sat in the hotel restaurant.

I had memorized Liam's telephone number earlier, and I debated now whether I should try to call him using the hotel phone. I'd felt drawn to Liam, and he'd helped me in the past. But my current situation didn't mark either man, Cormac or Liam, as trustworthy.

I'd picked up a small folded map for tourists and was orienting myself to the city. I wasn't sure where I'd visit first. But Nora's words gave me faith: Belfast. I was here to find some answers, and I had to have faith that I was on a path toward knowledge that would be important to me.

The Grand Opera House was close to the Europa Bus Station and the train station. It was all in one convenient area. I realized I could have walked to the hotel instead of using a cab. I was organizing the information when I looked up and about choked on the pint of Guinness that I'd ordered.

It was Fiona, the private investigator from the solicitor's office, standing over me. How did she know I was in Belfast?

"I'm here to help," she said as she slipped into the cushion-covered seat across from me. As if reading my mind, she added, "You've no one else to trust. It's not safe to have an extended conversation here. There may be others that are listening. Let's find a place to get some lunch where we can safely talk."

Fiona took the menu and skimmed through it. "I heard a rumor of an American with a problem, and Mr. McDonough sent me to find you. When I went to Eyeries to follow the trail, your psychic relative, Nora, told me you were in trouble." She looked up. "Do you want something to eat?"

I couldn't remember the last time I'd eaten real food in a pub. "Seafood chowder would be lovely."

Fiona went to the bar and ordered. She came back and picked up where she'd left off. "Nora told me she'd seen something in your tea reading—a dire warning. I was able to follow you until the hotel. Then things got tricky."

"You knew I was kidnapped?"

"I knew you'd disappeared. No one at the hotel claimed to remember you. That's when I knew it was serious."

We'd gotten our food. I dipped my spoon into the rich, creamy broth. Suddenly, things didn't seem quite so grim.

"I got away by starting a fire," I said as I took a bite of my chowder. "And Cormac, the dead priest, is alive. At least he was when I lit the fuse in the bottle of the Jameson's. I don't know about afterward."

Fiona raised an eyebrow.

I told her how my troubles had begun after I discovered the rosary; I told her that I believed that Cormac had planted it on me that first evening when we met; I even confessed and told her how he'd kissed me into submission that night—before I knew he was a priest.

"Right, something…" She stopped in midspeech. The waitress had brought us brown bread and butter. When she was gone, Fiona started again. "Why is the rosary so important?"

I'd rattled the whole thing around in my mind for so long that I didn't have any perspective.

She handed me her phone. "Give it to me if Liam answers."

When the call slipped into voice mail, I left another brief message.

"Now he has *my* number," she said.

She looked quite pleased with herself. "We're off."

Chapter 20
History and Conflict

FOR ALL OF THE HISTORY of violence in Belfast, it's a quiet little city. It sports a museum dedicated to the *Titanic*, which seemed ironic, considering the fact that I felt like I'd hit a personal iceberg.

"You're going undercover as a tourist. While you get to know the city, I'm going to visit some friends," Fiona said.

"I want to see the underbelly of Belfast too," I told her. She smiled in her bewitching way, which I could see was an advantage as a private investigator.

"We'll meet in front of the opera house at five tonight." Jotting down her cell phone number on a piece of paper and handing it to me, she added, "Keep out of trouble."

I never try to find trouble. Trouble finds me.

Fiona disappeared down the street, and I pouted for a split second, until I saw a man holding flyers purveying tours to see the sights in Belfast.

"I'll sell you a ticket for the double-decker. Hop on and off. See the sights," he said in a spiel. "It'll be here in a few minutes. Buy the ticket in the hotel."

Just as I stepped outside again with my ticket in hand, the bus pulled up to the stop. Though the weather was a little chillier than it had been yesterday, I still opted for the unrestricted view on the top. Several other hearty souls were huddled on the plastic benches there. A woman got on the PA system and narrated the sights as we passed them.

It all seemed light and pleasant until I first set eyes on the peace wall. Nothing prepared me for that first sighting. "It's a wall for a war zone"—a shocked tourist said out loud what others were thinking. Graffiti dotted several stories of concrete—topped by metal fencing—topped by razor wire.

Oh my goodness.

My next biggest surprise was a vacant lot. Because in it, piled several stories high, were wooden pallets. They were topped with a British flag and painted blue and red. "That will be lit for the bonfires," the PA woman said. "Bonfires commemorate the defeat of the Catholic King James II in 1690."

Will there be s'mores? Sarcastic thoughts invaded me. I felt the taste of bitter emotions. Belfast residents in Catholic neighborhoods should be short-listed toward sainthood by the Pope. It occurred to me that it's a fragile peace in a city with peace walls, barriers, bonfires, and lots of self-control. And something was growing with each breath I took in Belfast, even though I couldn't identify myself as Catholic yet.

Keep your politics in check. This is not your fight.

I was American. American-Irish. But something was happening to me. As the ghosts of the Troubles haunted Belfast, the past was now haunting *me*. In this land of my ancestry, stones spoke to me. I'd seen myself in a past life worshiping at the altar of Mass rock and now feelings of revolt oozed from my DNA. It frightened and empowered me.

But this is not my fight. Psychic bipolar. I climbed down the stairs of the bus and asked the driver where I might find a more extensive history lesson about Belfast.

"You'd be wanting a black cab tour," the driver said. "Cabbie takes you to both sides. Stops at the murals and the wall. Stay at our next stop. One will be along shortly."

I got off the bus and headed straight into the eye of my ancestral storm.

The black cab was exactly that—all black. *Perfect.* I climbed into the backseat. "I'll be takin' you to all the sites," the cabbie said to me. "Call me Jimmy."

Jimmy ran through a quick overview of Belfast's history while he drove to our first destination. He pulled over, along with several other black cabs, to view the murals. "These are some of the more recent," he said. I looked at a painting of a gray-haired woman holding a sign that read *Ballymurphy Massacre—Time for Our Truth.* White crosses on a black background nestled next to a different woman on the same mural: *This Woman Wants to Hide It.*

Another mural was for the black cab tours: *West Belfast Taxi Association, 40 Years Unbroken Service.* Still another read: *Say No to Racism. Cherish All the Children of the Nation Equally!*

Amen. I felt the boiling inside me quiet to a simmer. But it still burned.

To the left of the cab was the mural for Father Alec, Peacemaker. "Father Alec Reid was a mediator and peace broker between the IRA and the British," Jimmy said as he leaned against his cab and nodded to the black-cab driver next to us.

One mural, in white and black, contained the words *End British Internment of Irish Republicans.* "Maghaberry Prison holds hardline Republicans who are opposed to peace," Jimmy explained when he saw where my attention was focused. "Fifty men." Jimmy looked over his shoulder as if a real-life member of the IRA might be there. "Are you ready for more?" he asked.

At the office of Sinn Féin in Belfast, the iconic mural of Bobby Sands, an IRA hero, filled an entire wall of the corner building. I read the quote out loud under his picture: "Everyone, Republican or otherwise, has their own particular role to play...our revenge will be the laughter of our children."

Jimmy nodded. "He fought for the rights of prisoners. He wasn't a criminal prisoner, but a political one. He'd had friends in his youth who were Protestant, but then he was shunned. He joined the Provisional IRA in 1972 and died from a hunger strike in prison. In any case," he said, "I'll be having a fag and waiting for you."

I entered the Belfast Catholic church. Whitewashed walls highlighted the figure of Jesus, which had been painted behind the altar. Angels sat in the heavens above light, oak-colored pews. The tabernacle was set with the host and a candle above it; it could have been a Catholic church anywhere. But this one held secrets—good and bad—the confessions of people in revolt and fear.

But this is not my fight.

Only a few people were praying in the church today, so I was startled when I felt the warmth of another body as it slipped into the pew next to me. "It's lovely, but sorrowful at the same time?" Jimmy still had the aroma of tobacco on him. "If these walls could talk."

Sometimes walls do talk to me, and stones, and...

"Would you like to go for some *craic*?"

I'd heard that expression in what felt like a lifetime ago. Cormac and his spicy scent, his laugh, and…I shook that image out of my head. Jimmy was Irish, and Catholic, kind of cute, maybe a little older than I, but the day was young. And I was tired of running away from Irish troubles and ghosts. Plus, I still had plenty of time before I had to meet Fiona.

"Brilliant," I said.

He smiled and put his hand over the top of mine.

In Rock Bar on Falls Road, Jimmy ordered two Rebel Roys, which was a green alcoholic concoction touted to be available only at the Rock Bar in Belfast. After two, Jimmy was getting cuter; I was lonely, and getting shot, kidnapped, and running away is exhausting. The noise in the bar was increasing. It had grown late in the day, and more people were coming inside to watch the soccer game—or *football*, as it's called in Ireland—broadcast on the television above the bar. "There's music a bit later," Jimmy said, as if reading my mind.

Noise in an Irish pub is delightful. Speech is faster than it is in American bars, and no one slows down for an American tucked away in a corner across from a Belfast cabbie. I drank my Rebel Roy and decided that I liked the way Jimmy laughed.

A raucous yell erupted whenever Ireland scored points.

"Tell me about the O'Malleys," Jimmy said. He moved his chair closer to me.

"My great-grandfather immigrated to America around 1925, I think. I don't know much about it, except that my father always wanted to return and find his family in Ireland."

The bartender came with the third round of the green goddess of Belfast drinks. Between the crowd and the noise and Jimmy's warm hand in mine—combined with the Rebel Roys—I wanted to melt into my chair.

"He met a nurse. It's a story as old as time," I said as I sipped my third Rebel Roy. "Heavens, these are good. Is there alcohol in these at all?"

"Just a bit. I like your story. Tell me more if you know it."

"He was Irish Catholic and married a Scottish Protestant in America. Not a match made in heaven, from all the accounts my father told me. But my cousin Nora, in the Beara, is a psychic. Maybe it's called an oracle here. Anyway, she told me they loved each other."

Jimmy took both my hands in his. "Luv, in 1925, that relationship would have been a crime in Belfast. It's good he didn't fall in love with her here."

"I think they really loved each other," I said. Except that I thought I loved my husband when I married him. And that hadn't turned out well. Maybe that's the nature of many relationships? It's a short burst of passion, and if you're lucky, it stands the test of time.

My Rebel Roy was half empty. Or half full. It didn't really matter at this point.

Jimmy said something to the men at the bar in Irish. They conversed for a minute, and then he patted me on my leg. "I'll be gone a few minutes." I felt the heat on my cheeks as I blushed from the alcohol and the fire that was burning inside me. It was a cliché, but I was alive and had been through a lot. There was a round of screams as Ireland scored another goal. I finished my third Rebel Roy and got up and asked for a glass of water.

The bartender came over with one and another Rebel Roy. He smiled at me and cleared away my empty glass. "Jimmy said to take care of you."

I downed half the water.

When Jimmy came back through the door, he leaned in close to me. Again, I smelled the faint scent of tobacco. There was something else too. It's that scent that some men carry that's enticing. It's not cologne and it's not sweat—it's pheromones. The scent of coupling. The scent of love and transgression and forbidden passion. It's what you smell when you know you're going to probably regret it the next day, but you shrug and think *I'm alive, and I'll never be in Belfast with a cab driver named Jimmy again* and you want it.

"Want to go?"

Jimmy knew. He'd read my mind and my hormones. And for a fleeting minute, I thought about the nature of relationships. I hadn't given up on love. But for now, a warm bed to share with Jimmy was everything that I wanted.

I could have sobered up with a walk in the cool evening air, but the heat of his bedroom was where I wanted to be. Jimmy had dark hair and straight teeth, albeit with a tiny bit of an overlap with one canine. But he smelled so good. And that sexy Northern Irish accent. As he unbuttoned my blouse and slipped it off, he saw the angry scar from the bullet graze on my arm. "Bullet exited cleanly," he said. "You were lucky." He kissed it like that would make it better. "Jesus, you've a secret you've not told me."

I started to tell, but he held his finger to my lips. When he took it away, he kissed me, eager. And when my body responded to his, it was the signal he'd been waiting for.

I woke up with a headache, thirsty like a dog on a hot day. Jimmy was still sleeping. A tiny bit of morning light filtered through the bedroom curtain. I had that *oh shit, what have I done* kind of feeling like when you jump off a cliff without stopping to think about it. *How can I say goodbye this morning to Jimmy and…oh, crap, I forgot about Fiona! Holy Jesus, Mary, and Joseph.*

Jimmy opened his eyes and nestled closer to me. He kissed my tangled mess of morning hair. He stroked the side of my face. "Would you like to meet the Belfast O'Malleys on Falls Road today? Maybe ask some questions?"

I was speechless. Jimmy knew O'Malleys in Belfast? Could this really happen? That I might find my O'Malley family?

He kissed me again. I kissed him back. Maybe I didn't have to worry so much about everything. After all, I wasn't going to be in Belfast long.

But I need to call Fiona. That's going to have to wait. Jimmy was tender and loving. He was everything that I needed in my life right now.

With Jimmy at my side and the prospect of meeting lost family ahead, I had a permanent smile on my face. It was his day off, and I'd used his phone to text Fiona Kennedy. I hoped she wasn't worried about me since I missed our meeting. *She's not my mother.*

He stopped the cab in front of a nondescript house. It was small and tidy, but that didn't tell me anything; I tried to tap into any psychic feelings. There was nothing associated with any nearby objects, but I was feeling something from the way Jimmy kept staring at me and—I hesitated.

"Right?" Jimmy said.

I nodded. We walked up to the porch and Jimmy rang. Footsteps inside, a look from behind the curtain. The door opened. A ginger-haired woman, about eighteen years old, stammered and finally said, "Jimmy. It's grand. I wasn't expecting you." A look of recognition passed between them. "Bridget will be sorry to have missed…" She stopped midsentence, staring at me.

"Aislyn, don't be standing at the door with your mouth open. Will you let us in?"

Jimmy took my hand as we walked over the threshold. "Is your ma or da here? Or your grandma?"

Aislyn nodded toward a room. Jimmy held my hand and squeezed my fingers. The kitchen was warm from the heat of an oven. There was brown bread and butter on the table where two women sat, staring at me.

Did I forget to wear clothes today?

Jimmy introduced me. "This is Lizzy O'Malley from America," he said. "She's had a visit with a maternal relative in Cork, one of the O'Sullivans."

"Pleased to meet you," I said.

Two more chairs were brought over to the table. Hot bowls of stew came, and before I knew it, we were eating and laughing— everything that made it feel like family.

I told them about my brother, Ryan. I explained about Nora, my maternal Irish relative, and talked about her psychic abilities. I was assessing their general opinion on that before I went further.

Aisyln's grandma spoke Irish to me. After she finished, the room was silent.

"What did she say?" I asked Jimmy.

"Grandma O'Malley asked about your family on your father's side."

I explained the little bit that I knew, how my great-grandfather left for America and met my great-grandmother. That my grandfather died before I was born; that my father was gone, and that all I had to tell were the few memories that my father had left me.

Glances were exchanged around the table.

Jimmy spoke up to break the silence. "Aisyln's sister, Bridget, could be your twin."

With so little to go on, it was impossible to know if I was closely related to the tribe of Belfast O'Malleys, but it was highly probable. Grandma's eyes lit up when I talked about the Beara and Nora and my quest to learn about the psychic gifts in my family. "O'Malleys have power too—" Grandma O'Malley said.

Ma O'Malley interrupted her. "In thin spaces."

Everyone made the sign of the cross. "What's a thin space?" I asked.

"There's a story first."

I loved that about the Irish. *Best storytellers in the world.*

I sat back in my chair, the table in front of me filled with bowls of stew and plates of brown bread and people filled with contentment in life. I was warm in the kitchen with my new-found O'Malleys. Jimmy was holding my hand. I didn't want to leave, even though I knew I'd have to, eventually. Even though this O'Malley family might not trace to my great-grandfather, there was warmth and love here.

"It began with Gráinne O'Malley," Grandma O'Malley began, only a bit above a whisper. "She was born in 1530 and lived on the west coast of Ireland in County Mayo. She had a lust for life and the sea. And she had powers."

"Powers," I echoed back.

Grandma O'Malley nodded. "Powers. Especially in the thin spaces. She knew where time is thin because in those places, magic happens. Celtic lore. It's been passed down from generations that she married to build her land and sea power and fortune. She found places where she knew time was thin. She claimed she had knowledge of what happened in the past, even while she was in the present, and could foresee her destiny in the future. She could see and hear the clan O'Malley of the past, especially. Maybe other clans too."

Mass rock. When I knew I'd been there before. How I'd felt when I walked that path. When I saw the priest, or the ghostly image of the holy man, on the cliff as I walked back that day. But what about the stones?

"It was known that she had visions from a different time," she said.

Aislyn squirmed in her chair, discomforted by that claim.

I threw caution aside. We were talking about magic and temporal distortions. "Did the O'Malleys talk about ancient stones speaking?" I asked.

Grandma O'Malley looked at me, startled. "No. But if stones have spoken to you, have you talked back?"

Now it was my turn to be startled. It had never occurred to me to talk back to the stones. What a simple, wonderful idea.

"Next time a stone speaks to you, ask questions."

Like people talked to rocks, stones, and objects all the time. *Is someone going to haul me to the nuthouse?*

Jimmy had to work a double shift. Just before we left, he got a text from Fiona. She wanted to meet me, just like we had planned—except several days later.

"Well," she said as she looked between me and the disappearing cab with Jimmy inside, "you went undercover." There was a wry smile in the creases of her eyes at her double meaning.

"You wanted to see me," I said. My love life was my own business.

"Cormac O'Connor. Bollocks!" Fiona Kennedy, private investigator, polished and skillful interviewer, stuck out her tongue in disgust.

"Fiona," I said, "what do I need to know about Cormac?"

"He's no good."

I could have told her that. I tried a more direct approach. "What did you find out about Cormac? Is he involved in political factions? Is he really a priest? Will he try to kill me?" I asked my rapid-fire questions in the most factual way because I needed information.

She took a deep breath. It was midmorning, and though it wasn't something I'd usually do unless there was a recent death or pending funeral, I said, "Let's get some Jameson's—neat. Where's the closet pub?"

It didn't take long to find one, and I tossed down my first shot. I thought back to when I was in Sedona and had to go to the funeral home with a friend to make some decisions about a deceased friend. I'd tried to fuzz the whole event with alcohol, but that never completely numbed the pain—at least not like you'd wish. Somehow, I knew what Fiona was about to tell me would be painful as well.

"Cormac and Liam grew up in Belfast. Their da was a laborer. Both the boys took on more than they should at a young age, and Cormac, especially, fell in with a rough crowd. Liam and Michael weren't far behind. Some of their friends are buried up at the cemetery on Falls Road. The family moved to Dublin—then to Cork—for opportunities. Michael and Liam got jobs fishing. Turned their lives. But Cormac was terrified of water and never learned to swim. Cormac found his way through heroin, violence, and politics; he continued to run with a rough crowd. I'll not say here who is right or wrong. But the family held hope when he took the priesthood that he'd put the violent politics aside."

"But there's a peace agreement," I said.

"It's a fragile peace, Lizzy."

I thought about the Garden of Remembrance where Jimmy had taken me after I'd met Grandma O'Malley. It was a peace that could shatter at any time.

"There's something I want you to see," Jimmy said.

In the sunny afternoon, we'd walked in the garden where the names of brave men held a place of honor. Not graves, but memorials to those who'd lost their lives. "No graffiti here. The others know to leave it alone. Disrespect is tit for tat."

I thought about the heavy cab driver who'd delivered me to the hotel from the train. He'd gleefully smiled and bragged about the bonfires to come and how the smoke in the city would linger for a week. I thought about the wooden pallets, painted red and blue, stacked high into the sky in an abandoned lot, waiting for a match.

"It's a fragile peace," I said to Fiona, back in the present with a dawning of understanding. "And Cormac is still involved in some way."

"That's at least what others believe. Maybe something financial. Maybe something political. A financial trigger, I think, that will upset the balance of peace."

"If an antique rosary is the source, it's across the ocean now," I said.

She looked at me with a grim face. "I didn't think you had it with you." Fiona took out her phone. "I fear I can't keep you safe here." Fiona chewed on her lip as she worked through the apps. "There's a flight leaving tomorrow morning. It's Belfast to London. London to Philadelphia. Seattle and then to Portland."

I would still have time to see Jimmy and say goodbye.

"Book it." I wanted to tap my shoes together three times. "There's no place like home."

When Jimmy came by in his cab, he called me over and told me to climb in. "I've something to show you."

I was ready to tell him I was leaving in the morning, but I couldn't get the words out. He was like an excited teenager and wanted to surprise me with something.

We pulled up to the Belfast cemetery on Falls Road. I got a little queasy in my stomach. I've been told that I don't do well with death. "Grandma O'Malley said I should bring you here. She told me that it was a thin space. There are O'Malleys buried here, although most of that clan is still in County Mayo. She thought you might be at the end of your quest in Ireland, so she urged me to bring you here. 'Show her my people,' she said."

If the truth be known, I wasn't sure I wanted to converse with headstones. This psychic awakening I'd stumbled on in Ireland left me queasy. I'd been hushing the stones, keeping the stories from me. Now it was time to stand up straight and face my fears. But graveyards and funerals made me want to flee. I checked my urge to run, realizing that this was also about my ancestors and my past.

I kicked my toe in the gravel before Jimmy took me by the hand and hummed a lovely, soft verse of song as we penetrated the inner sanctuary of the cemetery, heading toward the clans of Irish residing permanently underground. We stopped at the clan O'Neill section, where Jimmy pulled some weeds around a headstone and signed himself with the cross. "There's my da," he said and pointed to Thomas O'Neill's marker. Looking at the dates, I saw that he'd died when Jimmy was young. In the afternoon light, I heard far-off birds still singing a cheerful song.

"Let's find the O'Malleys."

Not too far away, he found my clan. I went to the O'Malley marker and rested one hand on a tombstone. I felt like I could retch as all the voices clamored to speak, mostly to welcome, while some yelled for my attention. It was like a crowded room with dozens of swirling people around me, but these were ghostly voices from people who had once lived and loved. Uncles, aunts, cousins—a family I never knew I had, but who had been with me all along. Conversations grew louder and diminished. I didn't hush my clan, but after a time, I asked a question: *What is it that you want me to know?*

One voice stood out from the others. It was a woman's strong tenor, perhaps like the ghosts speaking in *Macbeth*. (Maybe the Bard heard stones speak too.)

Home. That was the message. I'd been looking for home in all the wrong places. My home was where it had always been.

I took Jimmy's hand. He'd smoked a cigarette, and he still had the sweet smell of tobacco on him. I gave him a loving hug and knew I had to tell him now. It couldn't wait any longer. "I'm flying home tomorrow."

He kicked at some loose gravel on the path. He hugged me again, and I hugged him back. Then he kissed me. Parting is such a sweet sorrow, but I could hear the clan O'Malley clapping in the background, and the strongest voice whispered urgently, "Home."

Chapter 21
Flight

AFTER THE CEMETERY, JIMMY TOOK me to a shop on College Square that carried outdoor equipment and backpacks. I selected a pack that fit comfortably on my back for the few items that I still had with me or had replaced while in Belfast: a single change of clothes and my few toiletry essentials. Jimmy gave me a few of his things too, including a warm Irish sweater to wear on the plane, which smelled like him and gave me comfort.

Now that home was coming into view, it was time to start my journey. My laptop had disappeared when I was kidnapped from the hotel. I used Jimmy's phone and left a message for my brother. I briefly mentioned my meeting Nora and my flight plans, but decided to leave out the other details until later. I didn't want him to worry.

In the wee hours of the night, after we'd shared everything between us, I thought Jimmy might ask to come back with me. But he knew and I knew that we had different paths. We said we'd stay in touch with each other when we parted at the airport, but we both knew it either wouldn't happen or wouldn't happen for long. We had separate lives thousands of miles apart. We each had our own homes.

After our final goodbyes, I still had some time to kill, so I looked for a paperback book. I found a vampire-fantasy story—*really, people still read these? Of course, look at me.* I also bought a black knit cap with the word *Belfast* on it. It looked like trouble. It was a good souvenir.

I made my connection in London, even with long waits through heavy security—many people were missing flight connections because of it. Finally, those of us waiting for the plane to Philadelphia were directed to board. However, when we got to where there should have been a plane, there was a bus. It took us to a plane in the middle of nowhere. After we boarded, I put on my black Belfast cap and pulled out my book. The woman next to me had taken a pill when we first sat down and was now lightly snoring. I didn't have one of those pills, so I buried my face in my book and read about falling in love with vampires. *Such an awkward relationship.*

British Airways serves good food. After dinner, I was given hot towels to wipe my fingers; then I went back to the pages of my book in the company of a plastic glass of red wine. The words started to get blurry. Time is different when traveling. I kept correcting my watch, but my body told a different tale. Dozing, I was jarred awake when the plane pitched and rocked with turbulence. The fasten seat belt light came on with the chime, followed by an announcement from the pilot, who said to keep seat belts on until we reached some calmer air. *The air is calmer here than in Belfast.*

Belfast to Dublin was a breeze. And the terminal in London is like a space station. Walk to the underground subway train. Take the train and hope you get off at the correct station. Follow the signs to the bus. Then, when you think you are going to miss your flight because it takes so long to get to that point, a bus pulls up and passengers load suitcases, carry-ons, and all the other accoutrements to an overpacked trip.

I think that flights going home take longer than the ones when you begin a journey. At first, the anticipation of new sights and adventures beckon a traveler. On the way back, it is more bittersweet.

In Philadelphia, I found a screen with the departures, found my flight and gate, and hung my head in disappointment. It was canceled.

I'd come too far to be turned away from home for another day. Desperate, I found the airline counter and asked for another flight because of the cancellation.

"Got to go to customer service," the agent told me.

"Where's that?" I asked. *This is one big airport.*

I had to walk nearly the length of three football fields to get to it. I was only carrying my pack, but everything was getting heavy. When I'd gotten to the counter, sweat trickled down my back.

"I started my trip in Belfast. I made it to London. Now I'm here and I need to get to Portland. Is there any way I can get there today?"

The customer service representative tapped his screen to life, and after minutes of key stokes and clicks, he told me he could get me to Seattle. After that, he had me booked on a connecting flight to Portland, but I would only make it if I could get to the gate in under twenty minutes and my flight was on time. Otherwise, it would be the next morning.

At least I'm closer.

The representative handed over my new ticket. Of course, the gate was back across the three football fields that I'd already walked. When I finally got to the gate, I dropped into a vacant chair in relief.

It was after I'd made myself somewhat comfortable and it was getting close to the time to board that I noticed that the screen didn't show Seattle as the destination. I went up to the desk and was told my flight had a new gate, so I hustled back down the length of one football field and made a skip-run maneuver to get to the new gate that had been assigned. About thirty people followed me.

Will a plane leave with thirty people still left to board?

With only minutes to spare, I found myself in my plane seat, ready for the next part of the flight. I'd been so focused on the run-around that I'd almost forgotten to be worried. As I cooled down from my mad dash, I felt a mild metallic tingle in my mouth. I was sitting next to a mom and her two children. They looked harmless. *Is someone following me?*

I looked around but didn't see anything out of the ordinary.

The flight to Seattle gave me back some of the hours of my life that I'd lost when I traveled in the other direction to Ireland. My mouth took on that feel it did when I was traveling, but I knew I'd be lucky to make the connection, much less have time to dash into the airport bathroom and brush my teeth.

Luckily, the gates were almost next to each other, so when we landed in Seattle, it only took a few minutes to get to the flight I needed to board for Portland. *On time.* I even had a chance to go over to a kiosk and buy a cup of Seattle's Best coffee for the flight. I would have brushed my teeth, but the bathroom was too far away.

The flight between Seattle and Portland was an Alaska puddle jumper—tiny seats, two by two on both sides, two flight attendants, and thirty minutes of air. When I looked out the window, it was dark—until we reached Portland, where the city lights twinkled below us. We fastened our seatbelts and returned everything to an upright position. I spied the dark waters of the Columbia River spreading in front of us, welcoming me home.

With a quick, two-step bounce, the plane landed safely on the runway and taxied toward the terminal. The flight attendant announced the local time as 12:03 a.m. and thanked us for flying with Alaska.

Exiting PDX, I queued up for a cab, but there was a long line of passengers waiting already. A steady but slow line of cabs picked up passengers. I'd lost track of how many long hours I'd traveled—it was about half a day as far as the clock went, but in reality, it was more like a day and a half. I'd gotten a little sleep, but I still had one more leg of my journey ahead of me. Luckily, no metallic taste in my mouth. No hairs on end.

Chapter 22

Home Again

THE CAB DROPPED ME IN front of Uncle Callaghan's house in Southwest Portland about 1:00 a.m.

Uncle Callaghan and I had reconciled our family differences after I'd reached out to him in Sedona, making a telephone call from the Catholic church overlooking the red-rock canyons. I'd sent up my forgiveness to all the people in my life who had rejected me and my brother, Ryan, and made my amends. Ryan was now thriving in Sedona; his Courtyard Theater flourished.

Ryan and I had discussed Aunt Thelma's house—the weathered, gray clapboard home in Manzanita, on the beach in that tiny Oregon town. We would have liked to keep it but had agreed to sell it, if possible, because both of us were too unsettled to move permanently into small-town life.

Then a moment of clarity hit me. Nora and Thelma had both found their spiritual needs met by the ocean. *Coincidence?*

I could hear my Aunt Thelma's voice in my mind. *Nothing is a coincidence.*

When I was younger and living with my aunt, I'd roll my eyes when she said that. She always wanted to read my tea leaves in the morning before school. Now I wished that I could hear her say that again.

My car had almost been totaled during a rear-end crash in my final days in Sedona. It was drivable, but it looked sad. I'd parked it in front of Uncle Callaghan's house to save money and keep it safe until I could buy a newer car. A bitter, cold breeze blew, and I shivered—not only against the gust but from the damp drizzle.

The hairs on my arms rose. *Wait. No metallic feeling in my mouth. What is it? Jet lag or a real threat?*

It was too late to disturb Uncle Callaghan's sleep for a nonemergency, so I left a note on his door that I'd taken the car. I pulled my battered vehicle out into the deserted street, determined to get to Manzanita tonight. I stopped for a cup of coffee before I headed toward the freeway.

It was an uneventful drive.

Although the fist rays of dawn had not penetrated the sky, I knew it wouldn't be long before daylight returned. As I pulled up in front of the weathered, cedar-shingled beach house, I spied Aunt Thelma's red Adirondack chairs on the porch standing like sentinels. As I opened the front door and smelled the scent of lavender she'd used to calm anxious spirits, I groaned. The loss of my aunt, the travel to Ireland and meeting my aunt's Irish counterpart, Nora, my collision of fate with Cormac and Liam—I collapsed with a heavy sigh into the velvet blue sofa in the living room. Now that Thelma was on the other side, I wondered if she would attempt to communicate with me, especially since this had been her home.

It was the rays of sunlight that woke me. I had been in such a deep sleep, I didn't know where I was when I first rubbed my eyes and Aunt Thelma's living room came into focus. I had dreamed of men chasing me. *Actually,* I thought, *that was pretty much what was actually happening until now.* Back in the calming influence of where I'd grown up, I felt at ease again, returning home to a place that I knew, a small town where people all know each other and care about your life. It was the first time in a long time that I'd felt that way.

I had decided on my first errand of the day, and that was to drive to the local bakery in Manzanita and buy some marionberry scones. (These pastry treats had centers filled with the berry that horticulturists created in Marion county, hence the name, marionberry.) I also was looking forward to a steaming cup of French roast coffee to go with them. With cream. From the local Tillamook cows.

Embrace where you are.

My second errand was more important. Manzanita is a coastal town of less than one hundred souls, and the local sheriff's assistant also worked as the emergency 911 operator. Not that there were a whole lot of emergencies in a town that size. On the coast people sometimes underestimated the sneaker waves. Or kids would climb out to a tidal pool in the rocks, only to get stuck once the tide came in again.

There were also volunteers at the local fire department who responded to a call. I knew them all, and they knew me. When I was a teenager living in Manzanita, I wanted everyone to quit watching me because I was angry that I'd lost my dad and my mother had abandoned me. And even though I didn't like cops, and even though I'd resisted Griffin's attempts to help me when I'd first moved to Manzanita, he and Trinity were like my family now.

With three scones in a bag in my left hand and a coffee in my right, I pushed open the door to the Manzanita Police Department and was greeted by Trinity. She was buxom, black-skinned, and had gray streaks in her dreadlocks. She wore bright-red lipstick today and greeted me with a grin from ear to ear.

"Look who came home!" She laughed. "Your dog will go crazy when she sees you," she added.

I placed one scone on a napkin in front of her. She nodded toward the door down the hall. "He'll be happy to see you too," she said. "He heard about that man who was your husband and what he tried to pull." Her hands were on her hips. "Griffin was ready to take care of things himself." She blew on her finger like it was a smoking gun.

"Did you get a package from Ireland?" I asked as I remembered the tiny post office in Eyeries.

"He's got it," she answered as she pointed toward Griffin's door.

Griffin lifted his eyebrows almost to his hairline when he motioned for me to step inside his office. At the same time, he opened his desk drawer and pulled out a package stamped with Irish stamps and postage marks. It was addressed to me, care of the Manzanita Police Department.

I gave him the fast version of events in Ireland. "Should I be worried?" I asked. "And if so, what can I do?"

"Why don't you open that envelope and let me look at that rosary?" he suggested.

I unwrapped it, removing the packing material that I'd carefully placed around the rosary while in Eyeries. It seemed even more lovely with its aged patina in the office light. I handed it to Griffin.

He took a magnifying loupe from the top of his desk drawer. "A new hobby of mine. I collect agates along the tidal line and polish the best. Loupe helps you to see things you can't see with the naked eye."

He put the loupe down and scratched at the whiskers on his face. "I'm going to send this to the police lab in Portland. I have someone coming to pick up a delivery. It should get to the lab right away. Something is embedded in one of the wooden beads. We'll let the lab people figure it out," he said.

Chapter 23
Trouble Continues

WOOF, WOOF! KARMA BARKED from inside Trinity's house as I stood on the front porch. Inside, eighty-five pounds of muscled, well-fed Labrador greeted me. Her wagging tail sped out the door; I put the key on the counter and locked Trinity's door.

It is possible, in the course of everyday events such as shopping for groceries and fixing up a piece of real estate for a sale, that a person can forget that something dark is lurking under the surface, waiting. Manzanita made the threat of the Troubles seem distant. I focused my thoughts on meeting Uncle Callaghan about Aunt Thelma's estate.

All was aligning in my world.

The drive from Manzanita to Portland usually takes about an hour and a half. It was clear and sunny the next day when I started out, and I was relaxed. My car had just topped the crest of the Coast Range. This stretch of road is filled with big Douglas fir trees that line the freeway corridor. My coffee was about finished. I was debating whether to stop for a restroom or to keep driving. I decided on the latter.

I looked in my rearview mirror and watched as a black Ford F150 crested the ridge behind me. The driver was accelerating, like he wanted to pass me.

But the truck didn't pass me. It kept getting closer and closer until I could see the driver's hooded head in my rearview mirror. Chills ran down my spine. Every part of my body felt as if it was being pricked with needles. A sharp, pungent metallic taste burned in my mouth. And then the truck's front bumper hit the crunched back end of my car.

Why won't people leave me alone? And my car too!

If I hit the brakes, I would die from the impact. The only remedy was to speed up, but as I faced the twists and turns ahead of me, I didn't know if I could make the corners. The black truck caught up to me and bumped me again. This went on—I would speed up and he would back off; however, it was almost impossible to control the car now, and I was approaching some deep ravines.

I'm going to die!

That's when I saw the lights of a state police cruiser behind the truck, and with a *whoop, whoop* hail, it ordered the truck to pull over.

I was able to slow down and escaped over the next crest. Even as I did, I smelled the sweet smell of lavender, as if a sprig of the scented herb was in my car.

Aunt Thelma. It was the scent from her house—the scent she used to calm me.

"Thank you," I said. "And Jesus, Mary, and Joseph."

Chapter 24

Tines in Portland

Downtown Portland, Oregon, is a mixture of business, retail, and homelessness. It's an organism of social commentary and commerce. My Uncle Callaghan, a powerhouse attorney, wanted me to discuss the last of my responsibilities regarding my aunt's estate. He also wanted to discuss the demise of my husband—and thank God he was dead.

I'd arrived in Portland ahead of schedule—not surprising, with someone in a black truck trying to kill me. I put Karma on her leash and walked her for a while to wind down from my drive and the brush with death.

She peed in the park, and we walked by the Thompson Elk statue—a 115-year-old landmark in Portland. Horses, dogs, goats, and people used to drink the water from the statue's basin when Portland was called Stumptown. From there, we walked to a doggie day care in inner Northwest Portland, so I'd be able to run the rest of my errands without Karma and she'd get a chance to socialize with other dogs. Karma gave me a resigned look after I turned to leave her. "I'll be back soon," I said. All was forgotten when she got distracted by a handsome German shepherd.

I still had some time to kill before my appointment with my Uncle Callaghan, and I wanted some fish chowder and brown bread like I'd eaten in Ireland. When you get a taste of something you like, it's hard to resist the craving. I knew of an Irish pub in downtown Portland. It seemed like the best place to search for the seafood chowder I craved.

It was getting close to the lunch hour at Kells Restaurant & Pub. Men in business suits sat next to women in short skirts trying to attract the men in business suits—it had a hook-up vibe. At the moment, I wasn't interested in hooking up with anything but the fish chowder.

I sat at the bar. It was a lovely piece of carved wood with a warm patina from age. I felt a faint kind of vibration of past events from it. *Psychometry activated.*

No image of a person came through who might have a connection to that bar, though. Then I was distracted from it when the bartender came to take my order. He wiped a wine glass with a white bar towel as he smiled in a conspiratorial way; he was wickedly cute. He had sapphire-blue eyes (probably contacts) and dark brown hair. He spoke in a faux brogue. "What's it you'd like?"

"I'm dying for some fish chowder and brown bread."

Maybe I should take the words dying *and* killer *out of my vocabulary.*

"How about clam chowder and soda bread? Closest I've got."

I sighed and settled.

When the bartender brought my order of steaming chowder, I dipped my spoon into it, took a bite, and sighed. *Close, very close, to Ireland. Food can take you back to a place you've traveled before. The rich scent of broth, melted butter, rich cream, and the freshest fish or clams, seasoned with salt and pepper and maybe an essence of some other spice*—my palette was a computer as I analyzed the flavors and textures of the chowder—*little bits of potato. Lovely.* Very few seats were left at the bar, but the one next to me was vacant. Someone sat down in it, but I didn't pay much attention since I was enjoying my chowder. I did feel that there was tension between the man who'd sat down next to me and the bartender. *Male hormones and bravado?*

The man next to me ordered the chowder too. That's when the hairs on my arm twitched.

My psychic alarm.

All hairs of both arms stood on end. *Warning!*

The man turned toward me, and I looked back at piercing blue eyes. A moment of awakening. *Those eyes look familiar.* A faint taste of metal grew stronger in my mouth.

Now that's a very bad sign. And I need to trust my psychic alarms. But what to do now?

Since I was almost finished, I reached for my check and attempted to make eye contact with the bartender, but he was busy with another customer.

Unfortunately, the dark stranger grabbed the check out of my hand. "I'll pay," he said as he grabbed for my arm.

I wasn't in the mood for this. The last of my chowder now felt like a congealed lump in my stomach. I recognized this man's voice, and I remembered his piercing blue eyes. I winced as I recalled that godforsaken hole in Ireland. I looked down at his left hand, and my hypothesis was confirmed: angry red marks from fork tines had marked him like a tattoo. All the while, a metallic taste roiled in my mouth. Without a doubt, this was my balaclava-clad Irish kidnapper. It *was* the same assailant who'd stuffed me into that underground prison.

Control rapid breathing.

The bartender finally turned his attention toward me. My heart thumped so hard I thought it would pound out of my chest. *Execute some kind of escape.*

Damn. I only have a spoon this time.

Breathe. My best recourse now was to leave—and fast. The man next to me didn't have a firm grip on my arm. I wrenched away from him, but he was too quick. He grabbed me by the arm again.

"Not so fast," he hissed at me.

"He's paying!" I yelled, so the men in business suits and the women there to meet them all turned their heads toward me. I shook loose from his grip and dashed out the front door of the pub to the sidewalk in front of Kells. I looked around to see who might help me. There was a person who appeared to be an addict with a sign in her hand, panhandling, next to a person in a sleeping bag on the sidewalk, asleep.

The man followed me out of Kells and caught me in a few steps. My back was against a parking meter now.

I'd take an angry meter maid right now. Never one around when you need one.

"I'll be taking back something that you have of mine," he said in a low voice as he stepped closer to me.

"What do I have of yours, *asshole?*"

The addict looked at me through her drug-heavy eyes. "Leave her alone!" she yelled.

I felt hopeful. *An advocate. I need one.*

"You abducted me from a Belfast hotel and locked me in an underground hole. Do you know what that's like?" I was beyond angry as I flashed back to that time, when I'd felt like I was being buried alive.

A woman wearing black yoga pants, carrying a Starbuck's coffee cup and a smartphone, ran over. "I've called 911, jerk off. Take a hike!"

The addict wasn't done with him either. She clenched her hands into fists, ready to fight.

"I'll be leaving," the man hissed at me as he looked between the addict and the yoga-pants lady. Even some of the business suits had come out to watch.

"But this isn't finished," he added, along with a vulgar slur.

No, it's not finished. I rammed my two-inch boot heel down on his left foot. I'd hoped to break bones; unfortunately, I didn't hear a crunch.

The addict shot a vulgar slur at him as she wobbled and spat on him.

As a Portland police cruiser appeared farther down the street, my nemesis fled, limping slightly.

I stuffed a five-dollar bill into the addict's hand. "Buy something to eat," I said.

"Got a cigarette?"

I put another five in her other hand and left before the police asked me any questions.

My uncle practiced law in a penthouse suite with a panoramic view of downtown Portland. I watched from a window in his conference room as a barge moved down the Willamette River. Mt. Hood stood clear in the blue afternoon sky. Uncle Callaghan entered the room with a worried face. Really, he always looked that way. Practicing law was a tough occupation, though for him, it was a vocation.

"Does the car drive okay?" he asked.

I nodded. "I appreciate the parking space. It saved me a lot of money. I would have visited, but it was too late when I arrived, and I didn't want to wake you." Though I didn't know if he really ever slept.

"And your Irish relative?" he asked.

"Once I knew she lived on the Beara, it was fairly easy to find her. Everyone knows everyone else. It's that kind of place. She even looked like my aunt. And the solicitor's private investigator had all the information that I needed to find her."

"Have you spoken to your brother about the house?"

"He's in agreement that we should fix it up and sell it. I don't want to live in Manzanita. And he's busy with the theater in Sedona, so selling seems like the practical thing to do."

Uncle Callaghan tapped his finger on the conference table. "My receptionist quit. I could use some help here."

It was a generous offer, but work in a law practice would be a jail sentence for me. Not that I didn't appreciate it; I just couldn't be at a desk for eight hours a day. And I'd hate to foul the reconciliation that I'd finessed with my uncle.

"I've got other job plans." I hoped that I didn't sound ungrateful.

"The offer stands if you ever need it." Uncle Callaghan smiled. Or at least one side of his mouth went up a little.

I still needed to get a cell phone. I knew where I'd get the best deal in Portland, but I also knew I had to maneuver around any giggles and snide comments from customer service. I'd lost my first cell phone when I plunged over a cliff in the Arizona desert. I'd lost my second phone in Arizona, when a particularly vile person stomped on it.

I took a deep breath as I entered the cell phone store on Alder Street. I started with a smile at the greeter. And then I went for the long wait. It felt like it took forever, but finally my name was on the top of the big screen in the lobby: *Lizzy.*

"What can I do for you today?" the woman asked at the cell phone counter. She wore a cute little blue shirt with a ruffle around the collar. Her name tag read *Sarah, Customer Service*. No last name. She smiled and suppressed a giggle as she read the notes on the computer screen, probably from my past cell phone replacement excuses, which included rolling over a cliff. My excuses were real, but they read like fiction.

"I'd like a new phone, please," I said.

And then it hit me. (Why did moments of enlightenment occur in places like a grocery store or a cell phone store? Not scholarly places like the library?) *Bam! The answer to this puzzle.* It was like a clarity bomb went off in my head. The answer to all of this was in a name. And if my hunch was correct, it would be in an Irish surname.

Chapter 25

Breaking and Entering

KARMA WAS EXCITED TO SEE me when I picked her up from the doggie day care. Apparently, her new German shepherd friend had been picked up by his owner. She was sitting in the corner of the play area, ignoring a small, yapping toy poodle. "Not your type?" I asked.

It's like that with relationships—they come and go—and there are a lot of people who just aren't your type.

"Here, Karma." She was up and ready.

We headed back to the car, past the elk statue. In a few minutes, we found ourselves safely on the freeway, headed toward Manzanita. Her playdate had done the trick—Karma fell asleep in the car almost immediately. *A tired dog is a good dog.*

I reflected that it had been a productive day in Portland. However, I looked forward to the comfort of my Aunt Thelma's house at the end of the road; that's when I realized I was ambivalent about selling it.

As I turned the lock on the front door at Aunt Thelma's house, the hairs on my arm shot up in a salute. Karma pushed her muzzle into the crack of the door and growled. I backed up about two feet. A metallic taste permeated my mouth. I ran back to my car and ducked into the driver's seat. Karma jumped in the car too, landing on my lap. Eighty plus pounds of scared Labrador was dead weight; I pushed her over to the passenger's side, cranked on the engine, and squealed the tires. I made a U-turn and drove to Griffin's office. Trinity was blowing the steam off a hot espresso when I walked through the door.

"Lizzy! Griffin's looking for you!"

He greeted me in the lobby and ushered me into his inner office. "News from the police lab in Portland." Griffin rubbed his chin. He had some stubble of growth on his face. "I want you to watch this video."

He turned his laptop toward me, and I watched a segment of footage from what must have been the lab's security video. As I viewed it, someone walked into the lab. Dressed in black, with a black balaclava, the intruder pulled out drawers and made a shambles out of everything.

"Did the police catch the suspect?"

"Keep watching," he answered.

Huddled over a desk, the masked intruder flicked a lighter and tossed it toward some paper files. The next thing I saw, smoke filled the room. That was the end of the footage.

"When the fire department came, along with the police, the suspect was gone. The police think that the break-in was specific to the rosary."

Same build. Same black outfit. My Irish kidnapper. He had to have been after the rosary; I was sure of it.

"The police lab agreed to return the rosary, without the chip," Griffin said. "They plan to send the chip later."

I stifled a shiver. "That's why I'm here. I think someone is in Aunt Thelma's house right now."

"Why didn't you say something sooner?" Griffin said with a sharp look.

The lab had discovered an RFID microchip embedded in the rosary. Griffin gave me some background about it. RFID means Radio Frequency Identification Device. It's the same kind of chip that is embedded in dog tags and credit cards. Also used in Oyster cards—London's subway system—the chips are rewritable. Inside these tiny chips, small amounts of data can be stored and downloaded. Some people, called "grinders," take the chips from cards and embed the chips in their bodies. By doing so, they can open doors without a key. Their bodies become the chip—if the person is able to coat the chip with silicon so their body doesn't reject it. Griffin speculated that embedding it in an object, such as the wood in a rosary bead, would be a handy way for a priest to keep the chip with him without much question; he'd be able to pass it on to someone else, and Griffin speculated that, most likely, Cormac had planted it on me. Maybe we had been followed that night in Ireland?

With keys in hand, ready to open the door of Aunt Thelma's house, I collected myself; Griffin was directly behind me. I could feel sweat drip down my spine. Griffin drew his service Glock as Karma ran to the door.

I slipped the key into the lock and opened the door. Griffin nodded and Karma ran past—*swoosh*. I heard her licking her empty bowl in the kitchen.

Griffin swept through the beach house before me. He came back to report. "Nothing here," he said. "But let's look outside," he added.

The beach house had a small, fenced backyard. Karma sniffed and peed in the grass, and then did her other business, after which she ran over to the bathroom window and whined. Griffin inspected the grassy area under the window. He put on a latex glove and picked up a cigarette butt.

"You a smoker?" he asked.

I shook my head. "It's an Irish brand," I said as I looked over at the evidence in his gloved hand.

"Carroll's?"

"Very popular in Ireland." I kept my composure as I thought about the number of times I'd been asked for a *fag* in Ireland—once in Fitzgerald Park when I'd sat with Cormac. The image of the twilight in the park when I'd watched the mother duck make her nest for her babies—it came to mind, along with the spicy scent of Cormac as he laughed when we'd gone for the craic…fun.

"That dark stranger must have followed me here. Maybe Karma scared him off."

Griffin placed his hand on his holster. "Maybe you should stay at Trinity's?"

"I have to get the house ready to sell," I said. "I'll be over here all the time working anyway. I don't think it matters whether I sleep here or not."

"I suppose you're right," he said. "But keep your phone with you—you got a new one in Portland, right?"

I eased some of the worry from his face. "I have it right here," I said.

I hadn't completely quelled his concern, but he also knew he couldn't protect me all the time.

Chapter 26
The Visit

GRIFFIN EXPECTED MORE DETAILS ABOUT the microchip to be emailed to him. For now, I turned my attention toward fixing up the house. As I sat on the porch with Karma at my feet, a little bit of sun came through the tallest trees in Aunt Thelma's yard. Catlike, I warmed myself with a hot mug of tea, wearing my wraparound sweater. Aunt Thelma kept it in my old bedroom. She'd given it to me as a birthday gift several years ago. A hint of lavender touched my senses as if she was on the porch with me.

I sighed. Karma raised her head and looked at me with her brown eyes.

I'd fixed up another house in what felt like a past life. With my inheritance from my father's estate, I'd poured money into the house that I shared with my husband in Portland. I thought I was happily married, until I came home and caught my husband copulating with another woman between my Egyptian cotton sheets.

I sighed as a car pulled up in front of the house. "What do you think, Karma?"

Out of the car sprang my brother, Ryan. I ran down the steps and threw myself into his arms.

"Surprise," he said.

I eyed him suspiciously. "What's the matter? Why aren't you at the theater?"

He laughed at me. "I'm taking a break, Lizzy. I wanted to surprise you, and I brought my elbow grease." He flexed a bicep. My brother had a keen eye for details, and I was grateful for both his strength and his artistic eye for design. That was what made theater staging work so well for him.

We sat down at the kitchen's yellow Formica table with a swirling '50s twirl pattern and chrome legs with matching chairs. Ryan looked around him. "It feels like a time warp."

I found a lot of comfort in the retro, vintage character of the house, but I wasn't sure if a prospective buyer would be so keen on it. "I've a few ideas to perk up the kitchen. I planned to get some paint and other supplies in Seaside tomorrow."

"What's first?" he asked as he rolled up his sleeves.

"I was thinking that the floor in here should be the first renovation. I'm not sure what to do, however. And some paint on the walls."

"Something bright on the walls. How about a black-and-white tile floor? And yellow-gold painted walls?"

I could see the sunflower color in the room. "Perfect," I said.

I refilled his teacup. I'd taken out Aunt Thelma's tea set and used some of her special tea. I'd been reading one of the books I'd seen on Thelma's bookshelf—she hadn't bothered to take it to the assisted living center when she'd moved. "Would you mind if I try to read our tea leaves?"

Ryan rolled his eyes but agreed; he'd moved away to find work in off-off Broadway shows instead of living in Manzanita, so he hadn't had the same experiences with Thelma's leaves like I had.

"Maybe let's wait on the leaves until later. I want to tell you more about what happened in Ireland and what's going on around here—including the parts that I didn't tell Uncle Callaghan and didn't want to leave for you as a cell phone message."

Ryan looked at me over the rim of the china teacup with mischief. "Since we're waiting on the tea leaves, I want to tell you about a particularly attractive Navajo by the name of Danny, who stopped by the Courtyard Theater and asked me to tell you hello."

I about dropped my teacup.

I'm done with him. "That relationship is over," I said, more sharply than I expected. "It's best to leave the past in the past," I added and promptly changed the subject.

The next day, Ryan and I drove into Seaside for paint, brushes, tape, tarps, flooring, and everything else we thought we needed to freshen up the house in order to put it on the market. As soon as we got back to Thelma's house, Ryan began painting the main living area—a sage-colored, spa-like green. In an hour's time, a storm brewed outside. Dark, gray clouds moved from the west with wind and finally rain.

We turned on the radio and listened as we worked. I smiled as I watched Ryan cut the edges of the paint on the ceiling. My brother's face was speckled with white paint like a robin's egg.

I was trimming a piece of tile when I slipped with the knife. The cut wasn't bad, but tension had made me careless.

I washed the wound and bandaged it. Ryan fussed over it. I gulped down Advil and decided to clear my head. I also wanted to get a walk for Karma before the storm hit. I zipped up my coat and clipped on Karma's leash. "Want to come along?" I asked.

Ryan shook his head. "I'm in the paint zone now. Maybe later."

"Big storm coming in," I said.

He looked out the window. "Even better reason to stay inside," he added with a smile.

Chapter 27
On the Beach

MANZANITA IS SO SMALL THAT people have to find ways to amuse themselves. Some people think that treasure is buried somewhere around town, where the roads are named for pirates and treasure, and fill their time digging holes, wishful for a treasure lottery. There are legends and lore that promote that sort of thinking. Karma and I were headed down the beach access path, through the tall dune grass, looking to avoid any new holes that we could step in, toward the gray Pacific. Darker gray clouds moved inland and rain fell. Karma found a nice-sized piece of driftwood and carried it in her mouth. "I know what you want me to do with that stick," I said.

It felt good to breathe in the salty air and clear my lungs of paint fumes. I tossed the driftwood into the waves, and Karma ran to fetch it. She came back and showered me with a shake of seawater and sand. She dropped the driftwood at my feet, ready for a repeat.

Back at the house, I took the old towel that I'd left on the porch to dry Karma. I didn't see Ryan or his rental car. I took off my shoes and dumped sand over the porch railing and unlocked the door. Inside, all was well. Ryan's paintbrushes were clean on the kitchen counter, drying. Next to them was a note. Ryan wrote that he'd gone to Seaside for more paint. I opened the windows to air out the house and went back to work on Aunt Thelma's kitchen floor.

I got into the zone of the tiling pattern, and when I finished, every muscle from my waist up ached, and my knees throbbed. It was well worth the aches and pains, however. I decided that I needed a hot soak in the tub with some aromatherapy candles and a glass of white wine. After that, I got into clean sheets. I knew it was too early to go to bed, but I wanted to read more about divining with tea leaves. I heard the rain fall on the roof, and I drifted off to sleep.

I woke to sunlight streaming into my bedroom. I peeked out the window and spied an elk chewing leaves. *Spirit animal.* The elk spirit is sensitive to signs of danger in order to survive; it uses its stamina to get through rough times, and it can sense danger. I let Karma outside and filled her bowl with kibble. I heated water on the stove and took the ground coffee out of the freezer. I put scoops of French roast coffee into Aunt Thelma's French press, and took out two mugs while I waited for the coffee.

I looked outside. Ryan's car was not there. Maybe he'd gone somewhere early this morning?

I'd slept so soundly that I figured I just hadn't heard him when he returned last night. I knocked on the door of Aunt Thelma's bedroom, where he'd been staying.

No answer.

Inside, the bed was made. I realized he hadn't been back last night. Dazed, I walked into the living room. *Maybe he changed plans?* I checked my cell phone; there weren't any calls. When I tried to call him, my call went immediately to his voice mail.

After the tone, I left a message. "Ryan, this is Lizzy. I'm worried. Call, okay?"

Still troubled, I called for Karma, slipped on my sweats, and decided to walk into town for a fresh blueberry muffin. It would give me time to think.

Walking through the cool morning air, I felt better. *At least the fog in my head has cleared.*

I was greeted by a cheerful hello from the woman at the register inside the coffee shop. After chatting a bit, I bought two blueberry muffins and headed back toward the house.

I decided that I'd wait until noon before I either got in my car and drove to Seaside in search of my brother's car or dropped by to talk to Griffin about the matter. Since he was the only law enforcement official for several beach towns, I didn't want to take the sheriff away from other work, and I'd known Ryan to get distracted before. He'd always been like that.

Karma lapped water from the bowl that I kept on the front porch for her. Her tail swished back and forth. But still no word from Ryan. I would just have to wait, and if I had to do that, I was going to stay busy. I was painting the sunny yellow-gold color in the kitchen when my cell phone rang. It was a number that I didn't recognize.

Please, don't let it be bad news.

"You'll not involve the gardaí," a voice said in a hiss. "I want the rosary, and you'll hand it over. If you don't, your brother will get hurt. I'll call again with directions. Follow them."

Before I could say anything, he hung up. *Asshole.*

Until I got the next call or set of instructions, the only thing I could do was get the rosary back.

Chapter 28

Rosary Roundup

As IT TURNED OUT, I'd missed my chance to distract Griffin, because he wasn't in the office.

Trinity looked bored when I walked through the door. "What's up?" I asked.

"Griffin's visiting the elementary school in Cannon Beach. He's impressing the first graders."

"Well, it looks like there are extra coffee and pastries." I opened the box. It contained an assortment of cream- and fruit-filled deep fried, doughy confections.

We gorged ourselves. Trinity loved her coffee too, and she'd already downed two cups. Sooner or later, one of us was going to have to pee, and that was the chance I was waiting for. I didn't like to go behind Trinity's back, but I had to have the rosary, even with the chip missing from it (that was still at the police lab). The chip had been embedded deeply in the wood, and I hoped my pursuer wouldn't notice. Besides, I didn't have another viable option.

It would be easier to apologize to Trinity later than it would be to deal with her potential refusal to hand it over to me. I was running on adrenaline and caffeine, and my anxiety for Ryan's safety wouldn't allow me any type of compromise at this point.

I got up first to use the toilet. As I walked toward it, I glanced around the office. *How long will it take me to find the rosary?*

When I came out of the bathroom, Trinity told me she had to go. "Would you mind covering the phones?" she asked.

"No worries," I said.

As soon as I heard the lock on the bathroom door click, I skulked into Griffin's office, having lifted Trinity's keys out of her desk drawer. By the time she got out of the bathroom, I was back in my chair with her keys safely resting in her desk, and I was stuffing another pastry in my mouth.

"You don't usually toss back the sweets," she said, suspicion aroused.

"Getting my period," I said.

"Can't get enough chocolate when I'm that way."

Chewing the last doughnut, I headed toward the door. "Got to go," I said with a little parade wave.

"Wait!" she snapped. "What should I tell Griffin?"

"Tell him I dropped by to say hello."

The next call came shortly after I'd arrived home. The man's voice was clipped as he gave the instructions. I was to meet him at the Astoria Column at 9:00 p.m.

"Come alone," he warned me. I knew that he meant it.

Highway 101 hugs the Oregon coast as you drive toward Astoria. Some views take a person's breath away. I hoped this errand wouldn't mean the literal end of my breath. I checked my rearview mirror, but no Ford trucks appeared in it. The drive kept me focused. I knew it wouldn't take much to nudge me over a cliff into the cold gray Pacific below.

The Astoria Column is painted to record historic events in Oregon. Time, saltwater, and air had taken a toll on it, and it was currently in the middle of a renovation. Scaffolding encircled the structure; now it was closed to the public. The visitors' center, used for purchasing tickets, was boarded up. When the column was open, visitors were able to climb a metal, spiral staircase. The reward for the climb was a commanding and unrestricted outdoor view of the coastline and Pacific Ocean.

The parking lot around the column was deserted as I rolled up before the meeting at the designated time.

We got out, and Karma peed on a patch of grass and whined.

Has she caught Ryan's scent?

My cell phone rang. "Lizzy, where are you?" Griffin yelled. He must have discovered that the rosary was missing. Since I couldn't think of a quick lie, I hung up.

I was going to get a royal chewing out from Griffin—if I survived. I set my phone to vibrate. Sure enough, the same number buzzed. If nothing else, Griffin was persistent.

The buzz from the next number made my jaw drop. "Ryan," I screamed as I answered the call. "Are you okay?" And before he could even respond, I asked, "Where are you?"

A groan came from the receiver, Ryan's hangover sound. It's like a prehistoric mammoth groan. "I'm in Seaside. Only planned to stay for drinks, but someone must have slipped me something." It was really bad when he didn't speak in full sentences.

"You're safe in Seaside?"

"Yeah, but feels like a bad night in Vegas."

"Listen, please call Griffin and let him know that I'm at the Astoria Column…"

My cell phone was grabbed away from me and then crunched between a boot and the asphalt. *I hate it when people do that to me.*

"No one," the dark bastard hissed into my ear, "is to come." His black balaclava didn't hide his menacing blue eyes. He grabbed me around my arms, and I struggled before I screamed, "Let me go!"

Under the historic events depicting Oregon's past on the Astoria Column, he effortlessly made the entrance door yield while he carried me. *Too strong.* Construction debris dotted the interior lobby, but no one was around to help.

Deserted.

He carried me toward a spiral flight of stairs. Up at the top, when he finally put me down, he jabbed a gun into the small of my back. That got my attention.

Karma whined at the bottom of the stairs. It was too narrow of a spiral, without any risers between the stairs, for her to climb.

At the top, a railing was all that separated me from a deadly fall. *I could be a spot on the pavement soon.* The bastard pushed me toward the edge until my back felt the cold, metal railing. I hoped that the railing would hold.

Another dark figure stepped from the shadows. *I know that spicy scent.* Even in the dim light, Cormac's handsome Irish looks momentarily quelled my fear.

"You've something of mine," he hissed. *I can almost see a forked tongue.*

"I'm sorry you didn't die in that godforsaken hole."

"Is that any way to be talking?"

"Priests aren't supposed to French kiss Americans on holiday."

I remembered that night in the evening light at Fitzgerald Park. It wasn't the same man in front of me now. There was an evil twist beneath the thin veneer of his personality.

"A priest, bollocks," he said with a sneer. "I'm going to enjoy looking for the rosary," he added as his fingers brushed across my chest.

"Oh, get on with it." This was from the dark accomplice, watching.

"Check the dog and watch the door below," Cormac ordered.

As the dark accomplice turned to leave and I heard the first of his footsteps as he descended, I yelled, "You leave my dog out of this."

Cormac reached my waist with his groping hands. "I don't think you're cut out for the priesthood," I snapped. I kept my eyes locked on Cormac.

I planned to kick him in his bollocks, but he'd disabled me by duct taping my legs together. He also disarmed me, throwing my pocketknife and pepper spray over the edge of the column, and took two steps back to survey his work.

It's not going well for me. My heart dropped into my stomach.

Cormac lit a Carroll's cigarette and took a deep drag. "So, where is it?" he asked with a razor's edge to his voice.

"What?" I asked.

"Don't play me." He gazed off to the edge of the ocean. "You're luscious, Lizzy, but I didn't come all this way for your womanly charms."

The other man yelled to Cormac in Irish from the bottom of the spiral stairs.

"I volunteered to retrieve the rosary," Cormac continued, "because you wouldn't have enjoyed the others who were almost dispatched here. Although the man down there would happily slit your throat. His hand still bothers him from where you stabbed him with a fork. So where is it, Lizzy? Give it to me, and you can go back to your *simple* life."

The judgment in his voice when he said *simple* irked me. And there was a look underneath his charm that carried the devil. I was on the bad side of some kind of deal.

"Why should I give it to you instead of the police?"

Cormac laughed. "Do you see the gardaí, Lizzy?"

He called to his dark accomplice to come up the stairs. "I believe it's time for him to talk to you. He'll likely throw you off the edge in the midst of the conversation."

I'd pushed down bile and consoled myself with the knowledge that Ryan was safe. And, after all, what they desired was taped to the inside of Karma's collar. The prize was within their reach. Stupid men should have searched my dog.

"Okay," I capitulated. "I'll tell you where the rosary is. But untie me, and I want your promise, with the Holy Trinity as my witness—Father, Son, and Holy Spirit—that you'll let me go."

"Done," he said.

He'd said it too fast. I'd overlooked something.

The other man.

"And that other jerk too," I added. "He's got to promise."

Back on the ground floor, handing the rosary to Cormac, I tried to recapture a little of my womanly dignity. "It would have never worked for us," I said with a breakup sniff as I slammed my car door shut behind me. My car started up right away—thank goodness.

Bless this car!

I drove to Highway 101 with a nagging doubt. I kept checking my rearview mirror as I revisited the situation. *Stupid!* I felt guilt at how my body had responded to Cormac. *Am I attracted to bad boys?*

I pounded on the steering wheel with frustration.

Darn him!

Clearly, my emotions were bipolar. And now I had to face Trinity and Griffin.

I groaned. I'd rather face down a murderous Irish faction than face the people who cared about me whom I'd let down. I reminded myself that it was because I had to save Ryan—or so I thought.

Ryan drugged? Is that how Cormac and his accomplice knew they could play with me like putty?

I checked my rearview mirror again for Ford trucks or anything else that might be trying to run me off the road. Karma fell asleep in the backseat. When I finally made the turnoff from Highway 101 toward Manzanita, I relaxed. I needed a shower, fresh clothes, and my game face for meeting with Griffin.

I stopped at a late-night diner and found a phone to call my brother.

"Are you coming back to Manzanita?" I asked.

"I'm driving now," he said. "Griffin called and confirmed that the Astoria police found no trace of the men at the Astoria Column."

The in-person meeting with Griffin did not go well. Not that I expected it to. Griffin was obviously frustrated with me, but I knew that he understood what I had to do. And, like a father, he would forgive me and help me to accomplish my mission in Manzanita, to transform Aunt Thelma's house into a desirable beach home—with the potential for numerous offers for it.

Griffin cleared his throat. "I've organized a work party for the house. I plan to help, along with a couple dozen friends from the Seaside Volunteer Fire Department."

With the extra sets of hands, the work went fast. I made sure that everyone was fueled with plenty of pizza and beer. I'd decided to take Uncle Callaghan's generous offer and move to Portland to work for him at the law office, at least until I could find another job.

"Pizza," I hollered when it was delivered, and I stuffed a ten-dollar tip in the delivery boy's hand. Griffin emerged, speckled in a mushroom color. He'd been painting Aunt Thelma's bedroom. Ryan had soft blue smudges as he came from my old bedroom. "Did I hear pizza?"

Chapter 29
The Devils Come Back

IT DIDN'T TAKE LONG FOR trouble to come calling again. I'd been at work at the law practice for exactly one week in Portland when I told Uncle Callaghan that I was going to be gone for a little over an hour for a lunch break. I'd seen an ad for an apartment downtown and was going to meet the owner. I'd been commuting with my uncle to work each day while I slept on a couch at his place.

I'd planned to meet the apartment manager at noon in the Alphabet District. It's called that because the streets in Northwest Portland are named alphabetically. It begins with Burnside and continues north. Many of the names of Portland pioneers grace the streets: Couch. Flanders. Irving. Lovejoy. Pettygrove. Raleigh. Old time, historical remnants of people who decided that Stumptown—the name for Portland before it won its current title with a coin toss by Pettygrove—was home. On Marshall, off of 21st Street, an old, stately house had been converted into apartments. And, for a little more of a deposit, they were *pet-friendly* apartments. I walked into the courtyard and waited, as that's where the apartment manager and I had arranged to meet. It was a lovely, sunny day, and it was nice to feel the warmth on my face.

The old house in Northwest Portland wasn't speaking to me, nor were any of the brick structures around it. I still had my eyes closed when the hairs on my arms stood on end. I groaned. Then the metallic taste was bitter on my tongue. I opened my eyes and saw a shadow move across the courtyard.

I really needed and wanted this apartment, so I dialed down my urge to flee. That's when the metallic taste surged as two men I didn't recognize, with blue-gray shadows of stubble across their tight faces, appeared in front of me. For a blind moment, I hoped one of the men was the apartment manager, but when I saw the syringe in one of their hands, I truly regretted my decision to stay.

That will teach me.

The other man grabbed me by the arms and held me. I watched as he plunged the needle into my arm.

When I woke up, I threw up. I was roiling on the deck of a boat. *Yep. A boat.* I puked again.

Damn them for sticking me with a needle. And where has that syringe been?

I felt like I could kill someone. But I had trouble keeping an eye open without the help of my thumb and finger.

A pair of new boots came within my range of vision, and I smelled lanolin as the river air wafted across the bow. It was combined with the smell of the gasoline engine, sputtering.

Lanolin. The last time I smelled it was when…

My thought was interrupted when the face from my lanolin memory bent down and looked at me—the Franciscan, Brother O'Mahony.

I tried to prop both eyes open and focus, but it wasn't working. I closed my eyes and tried again. Same face. I wasn't imaging it. I remembered how I felt when I'd been tended to by him. Powerful drugs—enough to take out sheep, people, and especially me!

"Oh my goodness," I said because I didn't think I should blaspheme in front of a Franciscan brother—even though I knew that he was no good. "It was you all along." With a kind of satisfaction reserved for the times I would raise my hand in class and get the correct answer, I settled down into a peaceful sleep on the deck of the boat. The Franciscan had other plans.

"Get her coffee," he ordered. Since opening both eyes was making me dizzy, I kept both closed.

"Leave me alone," I groaned. "I'm tired of you. I didn't ask for you to mess up my life."

"I want the chip." He was short and to the point.

"You have my blood on your needle, my barf on your boots, and my holy confession. I don't have it," I said.

The dark bastard grabbed my hair by the ponytail and pulled half of my body into an upright position.

"Ouch! Stop, stop, *stop!*" I screamed.

Propped against the side of the boat, I discovered that the rolling of the wake did not help settle my stomach. A cup of hot coffee was thrust at me.

"What's in here?" I was tired of sheep downers.

"Coffee and whiskey," Brother O'Mahony said. "It should counteract the effects of the drugs and clear your head."

"Hey, I didn't ask for a drug hangover." I was in a snarly mood, and I was up to my waist in a whole lot of trouble.

The Franciscan's eyes drilled into my own. I looked from Cormac to the dark man whose name I didn't know to Brother O'Mahony. "Cormac wanted to kill you when we found out the rosary was missing the chip," O'Mahony said.

I picked at a piece of nonexistent fuzz on my shirt.

"Maybe it's time to get rid of you," O'Mahony said.

"Wait," I yelled, "I can get the chip." I drained the contents and held out my empty cup. "More whiskey. All whiskey this time, forget the coffee."

O'Mahony sneered, but he filled half of my mug. I noticed that it was the same, high-quality, high-proof whiskey that I'd found when I was in my underground prison in Ireland.

"If I'm going to die, at least fill the cup to the top," I said, sarcasm dripping from every word.

"I'm going to enjoy killing you," Cormac said.

"Everyone keeps telling me that," I said, glaring. "And you're a priest. Too bad they let you into the inner circle."

Cormac reached down to grab me.

"Good, I need to use my legs. And to pee," I said.

As he pulled me toward standing upright, I took a brief second to orient myself. "I need a smoke too," I said to Cormac. *I'm being demanding in the last minutes of my life.*

Cormac obliged when he pulled a Carroll's cigarette from his coat pocket. He lit it and handed it to me. In the distance, I could make out the tip of Ross Island in the Willamette River. The river flows north through the city of Portland to join with the Columbia River. From there, it's a straight shot to the Pacific Ocean.

"So," I said as I took a drag to stall for a little more time, "what's your agenda with the chip?"

At that, Cormac grinned.

"Hey," I said because I didn't like the look on his face, "you French kissed me on my holiday. You're not in the big league of contenders for sainthood, priest."

The dark man inched closer to me. *Nerves of steel.*

"So, the chip will make all three of you wealthy? Or start a war?"

A fire grew in Brother O'Mahony's eyes.

"I saw a grave on the University College Cork campus. It used to be part of Cork Gaol. There was a headstone for an O'Mahony. I know your family had a part in the rebellion in Ireland. The clue was the grave marker on the university campus. I also know that you have family ties to County Cork, with your sheep farm, and that Cork is still considered a rebel county. I puzzled out the surnames and made the connections when it dawned on me about the family ties. I propose that you plan to use the information from the chip to usurp the peace in Ireland. It had to be something big enough to follow me to America. And I'm going to guess, if it's that important to you, your motive is all political," I said, addressing O'Mahony, albeit with only a slice of an eye open.

O'Mahony had the look of a feral animal. The dark stranger shot a look at him.

Ross Island is getting closer.

I turned to Cormac. "Pass me your lighter. My cigarette went out." This was my only chance. With nerves of steel, I touched the lighter's flame to the whiskey in the mug. *Whoosh!* It flamed like a Spanish coffee. And then I threw it toward O'Mahony and the dark stranger. I didn't wait to see what happened next. I jumped over the edge of the boat and stayed underwater as long as I could, kicking away from the boat, swimming like my life depended on it. Because it did.

The Willamette River is fairly wide, but not as wide as the Columbia River. I'd remembered what Fiona told me in Belfast—that Cormac never took to fishing because he was deadly afraid of water and didn't learn to swim. I didn't know if the dark stranger or O'Mahony knew how, either. The boat still smoked in the distance. After I made my final stroke to touch my feet on the sand of Ross Island, a hand shot out from bushy overgrowth there. Someone was hidden in the brush. And that someone was a woman wearing a bandana, faded T-shirt, and shorts. She reeled me in the rest of the way like a sturgeon on a line. My knees went weak and I collapsed, breathing hard. Recognition came over me as I remembered—she'd been in front of Kells.

River water dripped from me as my teeth chattered. She turned and waved for me to follow her up a rough trail. We went through brush and some patches of trees until we came to an open area with a ring of rock and a burned-out campfire. Hidden in the trees were a tarp and a sleeping bag. She had a few other personal items scattered around.

She shrugged. "It's safer here than downtown."

I'd gone back down the trail to see if I could see anything. I didn't want to be surprised, but nothing works out like you plan.

When I got to the edge of the island, where the bushes met the sand, I jumped. "You take a step closer to me," I said, "and I'll kill you."

"Already done." And then I looked closer because Cormac was—what can I say—dimmer.

What came out of the water from behind him scared me even more. It was like the river started to boil and swirl. Behind Cormac, a wraith-like spirit welled up like a vortex from the water, dark and grim. She came as an old woman, and she looked familiar—I'd seen that face when I'd been on the Beara, when I stood at the flecked stone of the Cailleach. Now the banshee-like Cailleach appeared with gray hair and a black veil that was etched into her stone face. She also had a black bag over her shoulder.

"She's come for me now," Cormac's ghost said. "I can feel her stone-cold breath on my neck."

The Hag of Beara…Nora told me I was lucky I'd seen her before. I don't feel lucky now.

My addict friend dropped the firewood she'd collected, turned, and ran. She'd only just emerged from the tree line. Apparently, she could see the apparition too.

An unearthly wail came from the wraith as it enveloped Cormac with the black bag until the entire ghost of Cormac was trapped in it. She tied it in a knot.

And then the sunlight broke through the trees on the shoreline, and both had disappeared.

"I'm not sure how to get back to shore. Is there a way off the island?" I asked, looking at my friend, hoping for at least a rowboat or a kayak. She caught my drift, but her form of transportation was to remain her secret. Instead, she changed the subject and pointed to the river. It was a cop boat. By the time the boat came closer, a familiar face greeted me—Griffin. He jumped off the boat and gave me a big bear hug. Not the usual emotion from the reticent sheriff. My friend had disappeared into the trees.

"You put a tracking bug on me."

"I knew they'd come after you. They found a body floating farther downriver. No one else was on the boat. Completely abandoned. Someone reported it smoking and floating adrift. It was stolen, by the way. And there's one more thing." He'd taken me aside and pulled a small envelope from his coat pocket. "Your property, the microchip. The lab sent it back to me."

I took the envelope and zipped it into my pocket.

Ancient people have tattooed themselves since Neolithic times. I decided it was time for me. It wasn't a completely random decision because I'd considered a tattoo before, but now I needed to find someone a little off the grid in terms of doing the right thing all of the time, since I had an additional request.

Griffin and his tribe of water rescuers let me off at the marina downtown as I had requested. Then I made my way into the darker part of Portland, off of Burnside into Old Town. I'd heard that Ronnie Parker, my first kiss in grade school, was working in a tattoo parlor in this part of Portland. We'd grown up in such a small town that everyone still seemed to know everyone's business. Not something I liked, but a reality.

I didn't have any trouble finding his tattoo parlor, as intricate drawings and pictures of tattoos in the windows graced the front of his shop. It was small, with an outer area where you picked the tattoo design and the color. There was a tattered cloth drape that concealed a second workspace. That's where I wanted mine done.

The door made a bell ring as I made my way inside.

Out from behind the curtain came Ronnie Parker. He looked much taller than the last time I saw him, and his chest was like a barrel. He smiled when he saw me.

"Lizzy O'Malley!"

"I need a tattoo and a favor," I said.

He waved me back behind the curtain and had me sit in a big leather chair where he worked. My resolve was diminishing, but I plunged ahead. After all I'd been through, it was surprising that I was nervous about a tattoo. I guess it was because I knew it was coming.

I rolled up my sleeve and showed him the scar. He knew what it was from. "Scar is healing well," he said. "But don't put a tattoo on it now. If you want one to hide it, I can do it later."

"I still plan to get one," I said. "I want a Celtic knot."

Ronnie got up from his seat next to me and brought back a book full of Celtic designs.

I pointed to one I liked. "A small one like that. Let's make it green on my lower back. And now the favor," I added as I bit my lip. "It's the most important part."

From out of my pocket I took the small envelope Griffin had given me. I'd thought about this: somewhere I could keep the chip safe but still get to it. It had come to me when I remembered what Griffin told me—that some people have chips implanted. Not legal, but that's why I'd approached Ronnie. I hoped he still had a soft spot in his heart for me. Or, that he could bend the law a little.

He took the chip—it was even smaller than I had thought possible; no wonder I hadn't been able to see it before—and held it to the light. He knew what he was holding. There was a bit of reverence or awe when he examined it. He took a magnifying glass to it.

"So, let me get this straight. You want me to embed this chip in your Celtic tattoo?"

"Can you do it?"

"Can and will are two different things," he said as he put the chip in a glass dish. He pushed it around a little bit like it was alive. "I'd have to add some silicon to it so your body wouldn't reject it, and yes, I've done it before, but that doesn't mean I'll do it."

"Ronnie," I said. "It's important."

His biceps were muscled and tattooed with snakes and runes. He scratched his head before he shrugged at me in submission. "I'll do it. You were the first person I ever kissed, and I still have a soft spot for you."

Chapter 30
Loose Ends and a Priest

I SLIPPED INTO THE CONFESSIONAL. I'd heard stones speak to me, talked to a ghost, and spent a torrential, hormone-filled night with Jimmy. *How does that stack up with St. Peter?*

Even though I questioned my faith, I felt the need to further explore my emerging Catholicism. The sliding door of the confessional opened. "Forgive me Father, for I have sinned." I signed myself. I recounted meeting Cormac, French kissing him and enjoying it, the discovery of his priesthood, an antique rosary that didn't belong to me, my sharpened and expanded psychic abilities, and communication with a ghost. I couldn't tell the priest about Jimmy. It didn't seem sinful. It felt like love.

"Pray for God's guidance," the priest finally said from the depths of the confessional. He cleared his throat and added, "And ten Hail Marys as contrition."

I felt a great sense of relief and accepted my penance. *I got off easy.* After my prayers, I looked up and the priest was standing by the altar.

"Would you like to have a cup of tea?" he asked. "I'm fascinated by old rosaries. I'd venture to say you had an antique from the penal times, when it was illegal for Catholics to practice their faith in Ireland. This shorter, abbreviated version of the rosary, with ten beads and one larger stone, could be concealed from view while its owner prayed the entire rosary."

I followed him into his office in the rectory. It was as small as a closet. The walls were lined with bookcases filled with books. Father Kevin Murphy pulled out a leather-bound text. Thumbing through the yellowed pages, he found what he was looking for and placed it in front of me. "This is about St. Adamnan of Coldingham. He was a saint with the gift of prophecy. It's not out of the context with the church, you know."

I read, "St. Adamnan of Coldingham died in 680 AD. He was born in Ireland, traveled to Scotland, and lived a life of austerity. He was known for his gift of prophecy." I looked up from the pages. "Are you suggesting that my psychic abilities might be considered kosher for Catholics?"

He smiled. "Perhaps," he said, looking as wise as Solomon. "It's too bad about the rosary," Father Kevin added, changing the subject. "That you weren't able to keep it, I mean."

"Do you think it was valuable?"

"Maybe," he said. "More importantly, penal rosaries are rare and should be in museums. The rosary kept the faith alive for years during the time of Catholic persecution, when it was a violation of the law for Catholics to worship, to attend mass, and to pray any Catholic prayers. And know that if the owner was found with it during those tumultuous times, it was a death sentence. Sometimes there is a date carved on the rosary, but there wouldn't be a surname. Most rosaries were a decade—ten beads—for saying the Hail Mary prayers. The ring helped to keep count, slipped from finger to finger. The other bead or stone was for the Our Father. In that way, the entire rosary was counted. Sometimes there was a cross on the end, or another religious symbol."

Even as I listened to Father Kevin, I knew that my time here, in church, had soothed my soul. And he made me realize that the conflict I'd felt between my Catholic side and my psychic side wasn't something to be ashamed of at all. My emerging clairvoyance and psychometry could be used to help people, as my aunt had done. I was ready to accept it.

I knelt on the kneeler of the pew before I left the church and watched the flickering candles of the faithful. I'd said goodbye to the priest, and he wished me well. I had to admit that a heaviness had left my heart after the confession, but I still needed to do something to put to rest the events of the past. I deposited two quarters for the votive candle, took the narrow punt from the sand, which was used for lighting the candles, and touched the flame from one prayerful candle to light a new one. This was for Cormac.

I watched as the light of the candle licked the shadows. Plunging the wooden punt into the jar filled with sand to extinguish it, I closed my eyes and prayed. As I signed myself with the cross, I heard the groan and creak of the kneeler next to me. I looked to my right.

It was Brother O'Mahony.

Crap.

"I will not leave," I said as I dug my feet into the church floor.

Under his coat, he produced a syringe.

"Not the sheep downers!" I screamed. Frantically, I looked for help. I saw a statue of Mary on one side of the church, a statue of

Joseph on the other, and Christ on the cross in the center of the church behind the altar.

"The priest is in the rectory. There's no one to help you. And you know too much. Your conjecture on the boat makes you a grave liability. Relax your arm so it doesn't hurt so much," O'Mahony hissed. Of course, I resisted, even as he plunged the tip of the needle into my arm and the liquid exploded from it. I wanted to scream, but nothing came out. I prayed for divine intervention; I hoped for a miracle.

When I woke up, I was on the carpet in the church. Father Kevin stood over me waving a nasty smelling substance. *Smelling salts?* He was an old priest with old ways. *Enamored of the past.* Around me were shards of plaster. As I looked around, I realized that my divine help had come when Mary—in statue form—was smashed over Brother O'Mahony's head by Father Kevin.

Sirens wailed in the background. My head throbbed, and I had a buzzing sound in my ears.

Father Kevin helped me to a seated position.

From there, the commotion was epic. The police stormed in, and both Father Kevin and I held our hands above us. Father Kevin, thankfully, spilled the story. I still couldn't string words together to make a complete sentence. I listened as he gave his account to the police.

The long and short of it was that without his help and the statue of Mary, I would have been kidnapped again. The police handcuffed the Franciscan and led him out of the church. A detective took our statements as the EMTs came in and checked my vitals. I was transported to Oregon Health Sciences University, where I was given IV liquids. I got tired of the hospital and insisted on my release. I signed some papers and had the information desk call a cab. From there, I went to Uncle Callaghan's house.

I'd been ambivalent about the beach house, but now I needed to act. I called from Uncle Callaghan's home phone and hoped Ryan would answer. When he was involved in a play, he wasn't too keen to answer. It rang and rang, and just as I was about ready to give up, he picked up. Breathless, he said, "What's up?"

"It's Lizzy. I've reconsidered on the beach house. I don't think I can give it up because it's home to me. I know it's probably too late, but..."

Ryan interrupted me. "I knew you'd reconsider. I haven't signed the papers yet. It's not too late."

I did a happy dance. "Really?" I squealed.

He laughed. "I know you pretty well. Maybe better than you know you. Do you think you're the only one with psychic abilities in the family?"

I hadn't thought much about it because I'd been told psychic abilities followed the maternal line. But then I remembered what I'd learned in Belfast. Ryan would have O'Malley intuition, of course.

"Uncle Callaghan told me that my bank accounts have been resolved and are secure," I said, smiling. "All that divorce and probate messiness is over. I'll send you a check for your half of the house."

Now the only other thing I had to figure out was employment. I didn't think I'd be able to find something in Manzanita, so I'd be commuting to Portland. Not impossible, after all.

The weather was still nice in Portland, but the hint of fall was in the air. The leaves on the deciduous trees started to curl a little bit;

the leaves looked worn. Soon, as the nights began to dip into cooler temperatures, the colors would start. Yellows, reds, oranges, browns, and faded greens—autumn in Portland. The rains would begin, too.

I'd run to Sedona to help my brother, but I'd gone because of the disaster of my now-over marriage. When I reflected on it, I realized I'd married too young and for all the wrong reasons. My mother was goodness-only-knows-where, because my father never would talk about it. And my father had worked hard to raise me, but when he died, I struggled. Aunt Thelma was my respite. She had been both mother and father—with the assistance of Griffin, who, in the absence of my biological father, had taken such an active interest in my life.

The waiter brought out two glasses of water and menus. My Uncle Callaghan was to join me if he could finish up his business in court. He was appearing at the Multnomah County Courthouse, not far from here.

I was debating between the seafood pasta and a Gardenburger. I figured I'd have to venture away from chowder since all the brown bread and Guinness made my clothes tight. I'd only glanced down at the salad choices—*boring*—when someone sat in the chair across from me. I looked up, smiling, thinking my uncle was on time.

I took back the smile. It was my Irish kidnapper, the dark stranger.

"I wondered when you'd show up," I said, calmly. I thought about the graves on the campus at University College Cork. I remembered when Aidan told me about the men who had fought for Ireland. I recalled the grave for a member of clan Moore.

It's all in a surname.

"So, you have some of this figured out?" he asked.

Because everything is like a Celtic knot, tied together.

"I think you know that I kept you alive," he added.

Yes.

The waiter came out to the table. "I'll have a glass of chardonnay," I said. I remembered sipping wine after Cormac and I met on my first night in Cork—my first night in Ireland.

The dark accomplice ordered a Deschutes microbrew.

"So, you're related to Mary Moore, my friend?" I asked as I took a sip of wine and peered over the edge of the glass to watch his expression.

"A brother. One of five. I'm Finnegan Moore."

I'd first thought it possible when I was at the cell phone store. I remembered the graves on the campus of University College Cork. That was my first clue. The Moores and the O'Mahonys and the O'Sullivans were connected through acts of rebellion in the past. Those same families, I reasoned, could be connected in the present. Mary Moore was my friend and like a sister to me, so she had protected me.

"Did Mary make you help me?"

"Her words were, and I quote, 'I'll have your bollocks for dinner if anything happens to her.'"

A smile eased from me. "When did she figure out I needed help?"

"She knew at Cormac's wake. The men in the BMWs. She knows politics. She'd talked to her friends and heard whispers about a rosary, a microchip, and treasure. The rumor is that it originated from Grace O'Malley, the pirate queen. That fiery woman buried her treasure of gold and weapons, and it's protected by fairy magic."

Finnegan rubbed the top of his hand. "Cormac, the rosary, and the chip found each other. A student found the key to the treasure in an antique book at Trinity College in Dublin. He transferred the information to a microchip. Next, it was rumored that it was held by a faction. Then Cormac sucked his brother into his rebel cause—a true codependency. You were simply in the wrong place at the wrong time."

I took another sip of wine before I breached the next question. "Cormac didn't know how to swim. How did he end up in the river?"

"O'Mahony. He was a twisted man of god, and he'd put up with Cormac for the prize of the treasure. When Cormac botched it—giving the light for the cigarette—he shoved him off the boat. I threw a life jacket, but it was too late."

I put my glass down and looked into Finnegan's blue eyes. He was Mary's brother, but he ran with a rough crowd. "So, what's your stake in this?"

"I'll not confess my politics. What I'll reveal is that Mary is my sister and she's my clan. She told me to watch over you, and I did. I'll make sure you continue to stay safe too. But I'll do it from Ireland," he said.

"What about the chip?"

"It might tilt politics in Ireland. The treasure should stay buried. And besides, Grace O'Malley put a curse on the treasure to anyone with ill will," he added. "You're an O'Malley. What better place for the pirate queen's secret to be kept?"

His final act was to hand me a package wrapped in brown paper, along with my laptop. *That's how they knew so much about me.*

"Can I get you anything else?" the waiter asked when he brought the bill.

My uncle hadn't been able to make it to lunch, so I paid the bill and left a generous tip. As I walked through the cool autumn air, I knew I had one final task.

I walked up the stairs of the church, opened the heavy wood door, and stepped inside. It was dim, but devotional candles burned. Up the aisle, I genuflected at the altar and slipped into the first pew. My hands were held in prayer, and I watched as a shadow moved across the altar. I recognized Father Kevin. He slid in beside me on the pew. As he clasped his hands together in prayer to join me, I slipped the penal rosary into his hand. With delight, Father Kevin moved the ring of the rosary onto his thumb and began the devotional prayers. I looked at his aura—it was a brilliant purple with blue fanning from his core. This was a man who wanted nothing more than to be a priest. He wasn't hiding from his past, or working a vendetta.

"Hail Mary, full of Grace…"

I left him to his prayers. The rosary had a new owner. In the autumn light outside the church, I breathed in the crisp, fresh air. I needed another job and a permanent place to live. Maybe I would find a job in Manzanita, or maybe I'd keep the house on the coast as my personal getaway. But things were looking up for me. And the best part about it was, I knew I was home.

Map of Ireland Locations

Acknowledgments

THANK YOU TO MEG EBERLE and Kaia Sand for hosting *Vignettes and Verses* in Cork and Glengarriff, Ireland. I'd also like to acknowledge my week at Anam Cara, a writers' retreat on the Beara. If you need a quiet place to write with great food, be sure to book a week there. Also, my special thanks to Mary Maddison, storyteller extraordinaire. She made me believe in the fairies (if I ever doubted). Much appreciation to Aidan Dunbar for the lifts, political history, and all around craic. And finally, thank you to Brian Reid of Belfast Mural Tours for the detailed history regarding the Troubles.

And a final note about some of the words and expressions used in *Celtic Ties: A Lizzy O'Malley Mystery*:

Speaking Irish: The language of the Irish. It is derived from the Gaeilge and is classified as a member of that family tree. But you wouldn't call it Gaelic in Ireland. It's the Irish language.

Ogham Stones: Ancient stone markers in Ireland, many of which can be viewed in a collection in the hallway at

University College Cork. Ogham is considered an early form of Irish writing, with a rune-like code that deciphers to Latin letters.

Lift: To ask for a ride in Ireland—well, if someone hears your American accent, it will pass. But watch a person's face and their sense of relief (or not) when you correct yourself and ask for a lift. A lift is a drive in a car. A ride is sex.

Craic: Pronounced like *crack*, it is derived from an Irish word and means fun, although it can be used in other ways. It's a common and frequent expression in Ireland.

Fag: A cigarette. One charming sunny day, as I ate my sandwich in Fitzgerald Park in Cork, watching the River Lee drift by, a teenager, about seventeen years old, walked up to me while I was sitting on the park bench. He was dripping wet, and his flip-flops made a squishy sound as he approached. He asked me for a fag. Without hesitating, I told him I didn't smoke. I wish you could have seen his face when he heard my American accent. (He was one of the adventurous souls who had jumped from a nearby bridge into the water. Probably not legal, but he was looking for craic.)

Garda: An Irish policeman, a cop.

Gardaí: More than one, i.e., the police. (Occasionally, *Garda* is used as a collective noun. Either is considered correct.)

Warden: The overseer of the dormitory rooms at University College Cork.

Blow-In: Such a lovely expression for someone from out of town—this can be someone who has moved from Dublin to Glengarriff, for example.

Celtic Tiger: The economic expansion that occurred in Ireland between 1995 and 2008, which resulted in over-built housing followed by a real-estate bubble bust, leaving many homes abandoned along the roadsides of Ireland. While things have gotten better, employment and jobs are still problematic.

Bollocks: A word from Middle English. It means testicles. In Ireland, it can mean nonsense, poor quality, or useless.

Solicitor: An attorney or lawyer. A barrister works with the court in Ireland. With her mild legal needs, Lizzy O'Malley needed a solicitor, not a barrister—that's what she would have needed if she had gotten in deeper. And then she probably would have needed the embassy too!

About the Author

A NATIVE OREGONIAN, KELLY RUNNING coaxes an appreciation for the English language into irrepressible seventh and eighth graders. Her poetry and essays appear in literary journals such as *VoiceCatcher* and *Faultlines*. Earlier in her career, she wrote commercials and press releases for radio. Her passion for research and interest in indigenous spiritualism instills authenticity in her storytelling. *Celtic Ties* is the second book in the Lizzy O'Malley series. More information is at www.kellyrunningmysteries.com.

Also by the Author

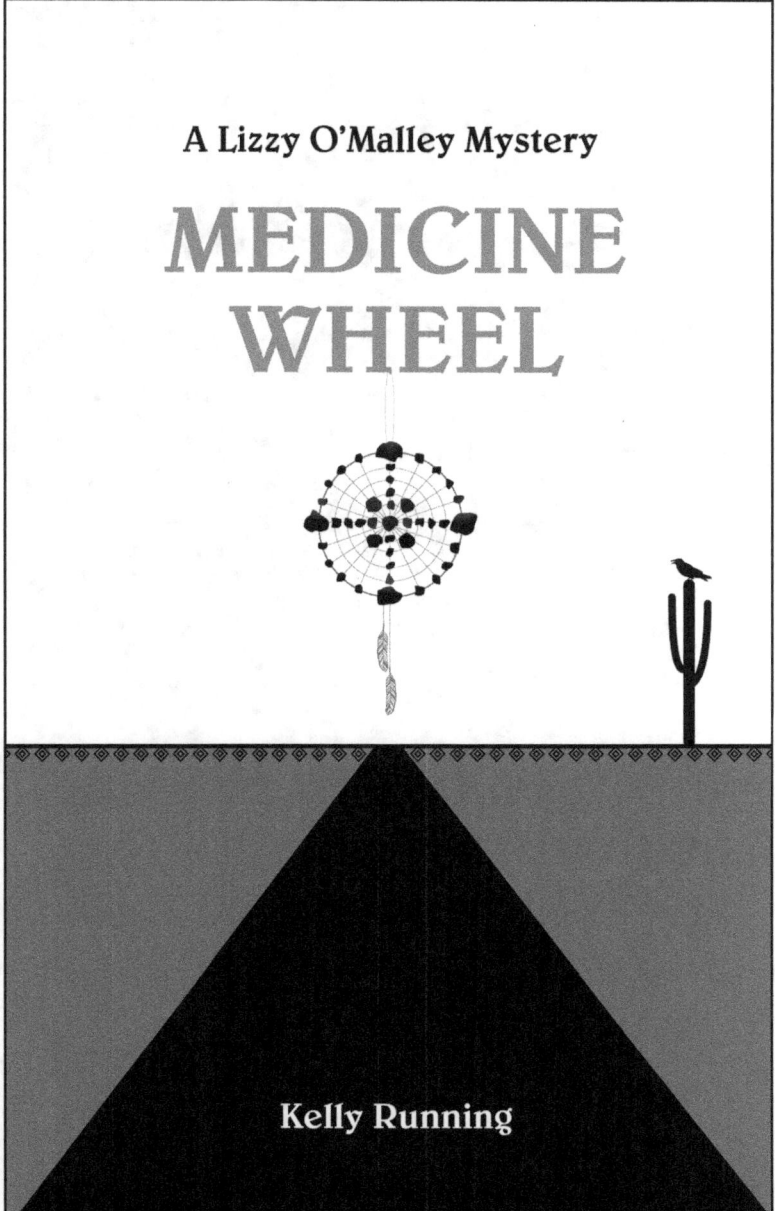

A Lizzy O'Malley Mystery

MEDICINE WHEEL

Kelly Running